And then the sirens went off . . .

Around us, the city went haywire. Drivers leaped out of bubble-tops, raced away. Pedestrians took to their heels like track stars.

"The alert—" Worts panted. "We must not be caught!"

We sped round the corner as a new sound made itself heard over the sirens and the mechanical voice that was telling people to go to the nearest Processing Shelter. I looked up to see jet balls in the sky, hundreds of them sailing over buildings, preparing to land.

Still running, we stumbled into a dead-end alley. Worts stopped, groaning, "I can't go on. It's useless."

"What's happening out there?" I asked.

"All must go to the shelters. There are . . . no exceptions. They will search the buildings, the whole city."

"That would take an army!"

As if my words were a cue, the sirens stopped. Then, from the street, the sudden silence was replaced by something far worse—the sound of marching feet, lots of them. . . .

THE HAND OF GANZ

A SCIENCE FICTION NOVEL BY
ISIDORE HAIBLUM

A SIGNET BOOK

NEW AMERICAN LIBRARY

Copyright © 1984 by Isidore Haiblum

Cover art by Paul Alexander

SIGNET TRADEMARK REG. U.S. PAT. OFF. AND FOREIGN COUNTRIES
REGISTERED TRADEMARK—MARCA REGISTRADA
HECHO EN CHICAGO, U.S.A.

SIGNET, SIGNET CLASSIC, MENTOR, PLUME, MERIDIAN AND NAL BOOKS
are published by New American Library,
1633 Broadway, New York, New York 10019

First Printing, January, 1985

1 2 3 4 5 6 7 8 9

PRINTED IN THE UNITED STATES OF AMERICA

PROLOGUE

The Control World governed the galaxies.

But not Earth.

Earth was off limits, in a still restricted part of the universe. The Galactic Council would never stand for an outright invasion. Even the Chairman—the Council's emperorlike ruler—wasn't that all-powerful. But with the help of a top-secret transmitter, the Chairman and his chief adviser, Pabst, had set up shop on Earth. That section of the universe was slated for reclassification soon; it would be up for grabs. The Chairman was getting a head start.

Pabst—through an outfit called McCoy—ran a network of agents, one that spanned the globe. When the time came, Earth would be a plum ripe for picking.

The Chairman, however, grew careless, was assassinated. But his memories survived, recorded on an XI tape.

When two Earthmen, Nick Siscoe and Ross Block, were inadvertently exposed to the tape, they found themselves in possession of the Chairman's mind, and the secrets of the universe.

But both Earthmen had their hands full just staying alive.

Siscoe was a brainwashed inmate on a distant

prison world. With the aid of fellow convicts Ganz, a master telepath, and Lix-el, a deposed prime minister, Siscoe escaped and reached the Control World. Only to have Ganz turn against him in a play for power.

Ross Block, meanwhile, back on Earth, had run afoul of Pabst. In a life-and-death struggle, Block managed to outwit the offworlder, using the transmitter to land on the Control World.

Block and Siscoe working in tandem stymied the forces of Ganz. But the telepath himself vanished before he could be captured.

Now civil war raged on the Control World. The Pabst network was still intact on Earth. And the Planet of the Dead—storehouse of frozen warriors—could tip the scales in any conflict.

The next move in the galactic chess game was up to Earthmen Nick Siscoe and Ross Block.

CHAPTER

1

All hell was breaking loose—again.

Sirens began to wail somewhere out in the city. Right on cue, machine guns started to burp. Block could hear the blast of a cannon from far off. Another power grab in progress. He wondered if this one would bring aircraft down on the Capital. And if the laser defenses were up to the job. He wondered a lot of things. But mostly Ross Block wondered how long this mess was going to last.

The gathering broke up fast.

The Galactic reps, party bigwigs, and their crew of hangers-on beat it for the safety shelter in the subbasement—a smart move.

The top brass ran off to gather their troops.

Lix-el, Siscoe, and Block made a beeline for the viewer hall.

The long plasto-deck conference table was left deserted; only piled documents, recorder tapes, note pads, joy-smokes, cups, and water pitchers showed that the table had ever been in use. The drill was old hat by now, almost second nature. In the seven days since Block had landed on the Control World, there'd been nine attacks on the Capital. And the opposition, it seemed, was just warming up.

The trio's footsteps clattered on the marble floor. They barged through a pair of swinging doors. The viewscreens were all dark. Block hurried over to the control panel, touched a knob. Different sectors of the city sprang onto the screens.

He twisted a dial. Magneto-ears veered toward the fireworks; spotter eyes zoomed in for a close-up.

The main screen was filled with men in gray-green uniforms. Their hands held lasers, blasters, stun guns. Some crude combat robots—refugees from the storehouse—rolled along with them. The robots wouldn't last long once they came up against the electro-scramblers. The men, Block knew, were something else.

"Recognize 'em?" Nick Siscoe asked.

"Of course," Lix-el said. "That is the center faction of the Unity Party. The League has informers in their midst. This move was not entirely unexpected."

"So why are we letting 'em run wild?" Siscoe asked. "They're gumming up the works."

"They are hardly running wild," Lix-el said.

"Could've fooled me," Block said.

"General Trig was fully apprised of the situation. The Unity Party has split into three factions. State Security and the General hoped that these internal conflicts might postpone any overt action."

"Hope blooms eternal," Block said.

"It was feared," Lix-el said, "that the Freedom Now Party would strike first. State Security has kept watch on both, of course."

"Sure," Siscoe said. "And on us too."

Lix-el shrugged. "You can hardly blame them. Your credentials are a bit hard to swallow."

"*What* credentials?" Block said.

"Yeah," Siscoe said. "The Chairman's mind saved our skins. If we didn't have the goods on all those babies—the generals, the politicos, the Galactic reps, the big money boys—they'd've stood us up against a wall long ago."

Lix-el nodded his large head. The skimpy hair over his bald dome was in disarray. There were bags under his eyes. His short frame and large stomach seemed to droop. The spunky former Prime Minister of Ardenya looked a bit peaked. "No doubt," he said. "But I should never have allowed that to happen."

"You're a pal, pal," Siscoe said.

On the screen the bloodletting was starting to boil over. Ivory-clad Galactic guards came popping out of doorways, took potshots from windows, rooftops. Copters dotted the skies, opened up with lasers. A swell place not to be, Block thought.

"See?" Lix-el said. "Our troops weren't quite napping, now were they? It will serve as a warning to the others."

"Don't bet on it," Siscoe said. "The locals here have gone blood-simple. They won't be happy till they've put the torch to the whole planet."

"Surely an exaggeration," Lix-el said.

"I thought," Siscoe complained, "you and your League had this burg sewed up."

"The League, sir," Lix-el said, "is holding up quite well, under the circumstances. We were hardly prepared for a major upheaval. But having infiltrated most of the governing institutions and almost all of the competing parties, we are in an enviable position to influence events. Our agents, however, must have time to do their work, to burrow from within, as it were."

"He's right," Block said. "We may have jumped the gun on this, gotten down to bargaining too soon.

The big shots around here think the planet's up for
grabs. They need some time to become reasonable."

"Precisely," Lix-el said.

"Maybe we should offer the party leaders a larger
slice of the pie," Block said. "It couldn't hurt."

"Sure," Siscoe said. "A little something extra, to
show 'em it pays to pull together. They'll catch on if
it's put the right way."

Block said, "Think you can handle it, Lix-el?"

"Certainly."

"Then why don't you?"

"I don't understand." Lix-el looked puzzled. "What
about you and Siscoe?"

"What about us?" Block said.

"Are you abdicating?"

"Uh-uh," Siscoe said. "Just taking a breather. The
leaders know you, Lix-el; they'll dicker with you.
Nick and I can come in near the end, help tidy things
up. Right now it's better we keep a low profile."

The little man straightened to his full height. "That
is quite a responsibility."

"I suppose so," Block said.

"Right up your alley, though," Siscoe said.

"Fortunately," Lix-el said, "I *am* qualified for this
task."

"Thought you might be," Block said.

"I shall call for a seven-day recess," Lix-el said, "at
once."

"Figure that's enough?" Siscoe asked.

"I can always demand an extension."

"There'll be complaints," Block said.

"Of course. But nothing we need fear."

Siscoe nodded. "As long as State Security and the
Galactic guards are in our corner, we're okay. And
those babies were the first we greased. We could've
sold their top brass down the river. Instead we gave

'em each a bundle. And a whopping promotion to go with it. They're grateful. This'll give 'em a chance to show just how much."

"Our agents in the various parties will preach compromise," Lix-el said. "And those leaders who remain obstinate will be dealt with quietly."

"By State Security?" Block said.

"Something along those lines."

"Just do it right, pal," Siscoe said.

"Rely on me," Lix-el said.

"We're going to," Block said.

Lix-el went off to the conference room. Block and Siscoe stayed put. Up on the screen the fracas was going full blast. A lot of citizens were caught in the crossfire. Some of the buildings were starting to burn.

"There ought to be a law," Siscoe said.

"There is," Block said. "And we probably wrote it."

"Like hell. Let's not confuse us and the damn Chairman. Just because we have his memories doesn't mean we're him."

"Just checking," Block said.

"Yeah?"

"To see if you're still you."

"I'm me, all right."

Block nodded. "Ditto here."

"It's like some fancy filing system. Everything's there. The Chairman's mind. The learning tapes. The stuff from all the XI cartridges. All on call. Some of it's still fuzzy. But I can usually get it into focus."

"It'll clear up," Block said.

"I know. Otherwise I'm still the same guy, Ross; just smarter."

"Better educated."

"Same thing."

"Want to be Chairman, Nick?"

"You kidding? Get tied down to this burg, spend

the rest of my life wrangling with the opposition, signing papers, trying to see no one sticks a knife in my back? You can keep it!"

"It's the top of the heap, Nick."

"It's a lotta crap. One headache after another. *You* want to be Chairman, pal, you've got my vote."

"Uh-uh. I'm with you, Nick."

"That's what I figured."

Block said, "So what *do* you want?"

"Damned if I know."

"Haven't thought about it?"

"Plenty. In between the shootouts and trying to get the beefs squared."

"That's about ten minutes of contemplation."

"Give or take a minute."

"Come up empty?"

"Who knows? Travel, maybe."

"The galaxies?"

"Sure. All that stuff's rattling around my noodle. Wouldn't mind seeing it up close. That'd be something, huh?"

Block nodded. "It's occurred to me too."

"Yeah. And Earth. Been away a long time. Kind of miss the old world."

"It's changed some."

"What hasn't? Look at us."

"We can't just take off, Nick."

"I know."

"They'd come looking for us. We've got too much on them."

"You don't have to tell me," Siscoe said. "Got any suggestions?"

"One, maybe. Lix-el."

"How's that?"

"You trust him?"

"Up to a point. Why?"

"He may be our best bet."

"Yeah?"

"We put him over, make *him* Chairman."

"Chairman, yet."

"Why not?" Block asked.

"Why yes?"

"He's a democrat at heart."

"Some democrat."

"His stint on the prison world's improved his character."

"That's not saying much."

"He's the best we've got."

"That's saying even less."

"He knows the ropes, Nick. He can make a go of it. Especially with the League backing him up."

"Possibly."

"It's either him or us. Unless you want someone like General Trig running the show."

"That's all we need."

"The Chairman," Block said, "didn't surround himself with nice guys."

"So what else is new?"

"The worlds that make up the Galactic Council are too far away to matter in this. Their reps here don't have much say. We need a good government candidate now. Lix-el's available."

Siscoe shrugged. "How we gonna get him the job?"

"Turn him loose."

"That all?"

"Uh-huh."

"You call *that* putting him over?"

"Step one. It's the simplest. See what happens."

"And if he can't swing it?"

"We pull some strings."

"You mean twist some arms."

"Uh-huh."

"I knew there was a tough part."

"So what?" Block said. "We've been shaking down the opposition for a week now, playing one faction off against the other. It's worked so far."

"So far."

"You have a better plan?"

"Nope."

"Well?"

Siscoe shrugged. "Okay. Let's give the old boy a try. Why not? Maybe he'll even put some life back into the Council. Wouldn't hurt, huh? So where does all this leave *us*?"

"On the Council, too."

"Yeah?"

"The Exec Committee."

"Where the action is."

"Yep."

"And all the work."

"Not for us."

"No, huh?"

"Uh-uh. We're just members at large."

"Just."

"That's the idea."

"Not bad."

"We drop by from time to time, help keep them honest."

"That'll be the day."

"The Council's a mess," Block said. "Everyone playing the angles. The planets won't be far behind. They're bound to want more autonomy. First thing you know, the whole system goes blooey. You get war, devastation, general instability. Prosperity goes down the drain."

"What prosperity?"

"Some of the worlds are loaded."

"And some are prison planets."

"Can't change the universe overnight. Have to go

slow—save what's good, junk what's bad. Do it in stages. Lix-el, if he becomes Chairman, will have his hands full."

"What if he blows it?" Siscoe said.

"Then it's our turn again."

"A two-bit hood and a small-time reporter are going to straighten out the universe?"

"Uh-huh. At least a little bit. We'll have some help, of course: the Chairman's mind. And all that hush-hush stuff he left lying around. That's our ace, Nick."

"Yeah. And we'd better keep it under wraps if we know what's good for us."

Block nodded, asked, "Any word on Ganz?"

"Nothing solid. He's been spotted a couple of times: the Security boys once, the guards another time. But he shook 'em. If it really *was* him. The guy reads minds. Tough to slip up behind him."

"All but impossible."

"Yeah."

"This Ganz is a menace."

"Sure he is."

"And he's good, probably the best there is."

"You don't have to sell me—I'm presold. The guy sprang me from the hoosegow, remember?"

"Uh-huh. He *knows*, Nick."

"Knows *what*?"

"How to get to the planet—the Planet of the Dead."

"A lot of good that'll do him," Siscoe said.

"Maybe."

"No maybes about it. The damn planet's off in a far corner of the universe. Without a transmitter there's no way he could reach it in a hundred lifetimes. And we've got the transmitters tucked away where he can never get them, guarded by a forcefield tuned to us. What's to worry?"

"Nick, if you had to, could you construct a transmitter?"

"Darned if I know."

"Give your mind a work out."

Siscoe's mind—like Block's—was the Chairman's mind too, along with a lot of other minds the Chairman had fed himself. Siscoe started flipping through a mental index file. It didn't take long.

"Son of a gun." He grinned. "You've got to hand it to the little creep, he didn't miss a trick."

"Except staying alive."

"Yeah, there's that."

"You find it?"

"Yeah."

"You're not the only one."

"So?"

"Look, it's all there in our minds—the works. If we could get it, so could Ganz."

"The guy's on the run, Ross."

"Doesn't matter."

"And it takes plenty of know-how—dough, a top-notch tech and lab setup—to build one of these babies."

"Don't underestimate him, Nick."

The viewscreen they were eyeing began turning red and black like a neon sign as one blast followed another. Someone had grown impatient, had brought in the heavy guns. Smoke and flames were everywhere. Streets, houses, and what was left of the Unity Party vanished from sight. Siscoe turned down the volume.

"Jesus," Block said. "Who told them to do that?"

"Sweet reason must've laid an egg. Some guys won't give up, no matter what."

"We could try and stop it."

"Too late."

"Think so?"

"Yeah. Except for mopping up. Ought to make the other factions think twice."

"At least twice. Well?"

"You're right."

Block nodded. "Sure I am. We have to defuse the planet, make sure no one can use those bodies."

"How?"

"Pull the plug on the freezing units."

"Rot 'em?"

"Yep. Or ditch the X2 tapes."

"Who goes, you or me?"

"You."

"Done in a jiffy," Siscoe said. "I'll hardly be missed."

"We ought to give Lix-el the opportunity of running things on his own," Block said.

"Now? In the middle of all this?"

"As good a time as any, Nick. If he can't put a colaition together with half the parties bought off and the League subverting the rest, he's the wrong man for the job."

Block reached out, turned off the viewscreen. The image and sound died simultaneously, was replaced by the far-off rumble of combat in the city.

He said, "I should go back to Earth. I've been away too long."

"Pabst?"

"Uh-huh."

Siscoe nodded. Pabst had been the Chairman's stooge on Earth, had put together a network to do his chief's dirty work. The Chairman was gone. And Pabst—when last heard from—was behind bars. But the network was still in place.

"No telling what those guys are up to," Block said.

He and Siscoe went through the swinging doors, along the corridor back to the conference room.

"This tape business won't take long," Siscoe said.

"I'll hang around here then, see that nothing gets out of hand."

"Fine. I'll try to wrap things up as quickly as possible, join you."

"Don't take chances, Ross."

"You kidding?"

"I guess I am."

CHAPTER

2

I stepped off the transmitter platform, looked around. And got my first surprise.

Damp concrete walls were on four sides of me. A small grimy cracked window near the ceiling let in what little light there was. The floor was littered with junk: a burned, foul-smelling mattress, broken pieces of furniture, a jagged slice of glass about two feet long. There was a door on the far side of the room. I could hear distant noises that seemed to be coming from somewhere outside.

I didn't like it one bit.

My destination had been the Planet of the Dead. This hole—whatever it was—wasn't it.

I rummaged through my mind just to make sure: three transmitter platforms on the planet. And all of them in more or less reasonable and sane places; their image stuck out in my mind.

The damn transmitter had misfired, no doubt about it; it couldn't happen, but it had. I heard myself curse. I had never shared the Chairman's faith in technology—even now when I knew what it was all about. This merely clinched it.

I wasn't interested in inspecting my new surroundings. I just wanted to leave this place, get on with my business. Ten thousand cadavers lay in stasis on the Planet of the Dead, ready and waiting to be activated at the touch of a button. Ten thousand Warrior tapes would turn them into a murderous fighting force. I'd dragged my heels, thinking I might have a use for them myself. But enough was enough. Time to torch the tapes, get rid of them before some unfriendlies stumbled across the Planet and wound up with their own private army, one they'd probably use against *me*.

I turned back to the platform, hunting for the transmitter controls that would whisk me away from here—and got my second surprise, this one even less pleasant: There were no controls.

I stood there as though someone had conked me over the noggin with a cement block and stared stupidly at the platform. Lack of controls wasn't its only novelty. The few platforms I'd seen before on my jaunts through the galaxies were bright and shiny. This one was rusted and pitted, a refugee from some scrap heap. Where the control panel was supposed to be—bolted securely to the back of the platform—there was lots of empty space.

I'd bought myself a one-way ticket, it seemed—to somewhere.

I made myself move, got down on hands and knees, took a closer gander at the damage. The bolt holes in back of the platform were covered with rust. Whoever had dismantled the gizmo had done so long ago.

I got to my feet slowly, as though his newly acquired knowledge had made me old and feeble before my time, and dusted myself off. It looked as if I was going to take the local tour after all.

I waded through the mess on the floor heading for the door. A large, crumpled piece of paper stopped me. It looked for all the world like a sheet of newspaper.

Newspapers were a dime a dozen back on Earth. But where I had come from—the Control World—they were confined to museums; multichannel viewscreens briefed the citizens.

Bending over, I scooped up my prize, smoothed it out. One glance was enough: headlines, columns of print, and even a pair of photos. The real McCoy, all right. Too bad I couldn't make head or tail of it.

Mentally, I thumbed through my catalogue of lingos and alphabets; the Chairman's mind was well stocked.

It took a while, but I was in no hurry now. Any clue to the world waiting for me outside would be a plus. A lot of worlds were a bit weird by Control—let alone Earth—standards, and some were downright hostile to offworlders. A little knowledge could go a long way in keeping me out of trouble. I didn't want trouble.

About ten minutes crept by while I poked around the Chairman's mind—now *my* mind. By the end of that time, I could almost decipher every third word. There my progress stopped dead. The local lingo was a hodgepodge of at least three different languages, all rated archaic. No reference to a new tongue growing out of 'em. That didn't figure. The Chairman had been no slouch when it came to updating his memory tapes. And he had kept a close watch on the worlds housing his hidden transmitters.

So what was going on here?

Hanging around in this dump wasn't going to get me the answer.

I made it over to the door, yanked it open. Rusty hinges screeched as if in pain. A narrow, moldy-smelling staircase led up to the floor above. I went with it.

The sounds from outside grew stronger. I hit the landing and found myself in semidarkness. It didn't matter. The place was empty, all furniture cleaned out. The windows were boarded over from inside.

I heaved at one of the planks, and it came away in my hands. I dropped it to the floor. Gray daylight drifted in. I put my nose to the opening, looked out. A solid, dirty red brick wall looked back.

That told me nothing except that the builder had been too cheap to use plasto-deck, and that I was probably in the rear of the house.

I decided not to bother with the front door; it would be nailed shut too—and less private. I pulled off some more boards from the window and after a while had a hole large enough to crawl through. No glass got in my way; someone had thoughtfully knocked out the pane.

I crawled over the sill, dropped to the ground.

The brick wall opposite, I saw now, stretched far off into the distance in both directions; it rose about fifty feet in the air. I couldn't spot any break in it.

I gave my attention to the house I'd just left. It was a dilapidated four-story log building. Identical hovels—weathered, unpainted logs, sealed windows, the foundations slightly askew—veered off to the right and left. Wherever I'd landed, it wasn't the Ritz.

I started walking. Twenty houses down I came to a narrow alleyway. I turned up this alley, waded through gravel, loose bricks, chunks of concrete, and presently stepped out onto a concrete pavement that had once been a street.

It wasn't anymore.

The pavement was all chopped up as if someone had taken a bulldozer to it. The houses which lined my side of the block were lopsided, ramshackle ruins. Across the street an overgrown weedy field stretched toward the horizon. Movement came from inside this field. I heard voices. Giant weeds and shrubbery hid the movers and talkers.

I glanced left, saw bluish hills in the distance. To the right, structures which could have been tall buildings peered out of a grayish mist.

So far, I'd learned nothing except that I didn't like where I was.

I reached for my hip pocket, slid loose the nerve gun, strode across to the weed garden. In a moment I was lost in what looked and felt like a miniature forest. I didn't let it worry me. I followed the voices.

The weeds began to thin out. Through them I saw movement, smelled smoke.

Half doubled over, I crept along, got as close as I could without showing myself. Then—very gently—I stretched out on the ground, poked my nose through some purple bushes, and took a look-see.

I was staring into a clearing. A couple dozen human-enough-looking men and women were milling around. I saw two large blackened pots, then a third. A fire was being lit under the first. I'd come just in time for chow, it seemed. I didn't get my hopes up: This crew wasn't about to hand out any invitations. They were a sorry-looking bunch, rail-thin, with tattered clothing that flopped around them as they moved.

I lay there watching this shindig and wondered if I'd landed on some poorhouse planet. Possibly the beat-up transmitter platform had been part of a junk pile dumped here in the regular course of events. It didn't seem too likely, but I'd know more when I found out just where "here" was. Watching these skeletal folks tramp around their clearing wasn't getting me anywhere. I took one last look to make sure there were no hidden cannons or machine guns to booby-trap me, and got to my feet. My nerve gun was back in my pocket, out of sight, but within easy reach.

I hadn't taken three steps when one of the natives—a bony middle-aged lad with bent shoulders and scraggly hair—caught sight of me. He let out a holler that not only froze me to the spot, but paralyzed most of his playmates as well. The old boy pointed. Two dozen heads swiveled as one in my direction.

I put a smile on my face, raised a hand in what I hoped was a friendly greeting.

I could have saved myself the trouble.

One look was all this crowd needed. They turned tail and ran.

I ran after them; it seemed the thing to do.

It didn't take much effort to catch up with a few of the stragglers. None of these birds was any great shakes when it came to stretching a leg.

I chose a girl as my victim. She had unkempt waist-length hair, looked to be about nineteen, was five foot two, and probably weighed no more than eighty pounds. Safe enough.

I put on a burst of speed, caught her by the wrist, swung her around.

None of her pals came to her rescue. The last one vanished into the shrubbery.

I growled, "Hold it, sister. No one's going to hurt you—"

She shrieked. Something that could have been words poured from her lips. It made no sense to me.

Fingernails darted for my eyes. I knocked her hand aside. She screamed, kicked at me. I held her at arm's length. "Listen—" I began.

She didn't want to listen.

More guttural, gurgling noises came from her throat; she was talking to me. I bent close, straining to catch some syllable that might contain a hint of meaning. Nothing doing.

I must have loosened my grip. The girl twisted

from my hands, spat at me, and raced off after her departed friends.

I let her go. I didn't think she liked me. Besides, all I was getting, in the absence of a translator, was a lot of gibberish.

I went over to the pot with the fire under it. The water hadn't started to boil yet. Some items that were probably vegetables and a pair of plucked birds were floating inside. They didn't do much for my appetite. I ground out the fire with the heel of my shoe, swung around, and trudged back to the street.

It hadn't changed any during my absence.

The hills were to my left, tall buildings—if that's what they were—far off to the right. There was nothing in hanging around here. The buildings seemed my best bet.

I sighed. And started hiking.

Somewhere during the second or third hour of my trek the clouds broke. A deep pinkish sky and a very large sun were overhead. Two smaller suns floated in the distance. They added nothing to my knowledge. I kept walking.

I had on a black jumpsuit with lots of pockets. Aside from the nerve gun and a handy utility packet I'd expected to use on the Planet of the Dead, my pockets were empty. I'd neglected to stuff them with sandwiches and water bottles. An oversight, all right. But then I hadn't expected to be shanghaied by my transmitter either.

I strode over baked, grayish fields barren of all vegetation, climbed over even grayer rock formations, and periodically brushed gray dust off my clothing. This place made Earth's 1930s dustbowl look like a picnic garden by comparison.

The tall spires ahead, which were now definitely taking on the shapes of some sort of buildings, guided me. I didn't get my hopes up. The city—or whatever it was—could be as much of a ghost town as the one I'd just left. And if that were so, the bunch I'd sent packing in the weeds could be a fair sample of the local natives. I didn't want to think about it. I was having enough trouble trying to keep my thoughts cheerful without picturing this world as my new—permanent—home.

My first close-up sight of the second ghost town did nothing to improve my mood. Burned-out houses greeted me. The streets had been blasted to little bits and pieces as though a crazed horde of piledrivers had run wild; only rubble was underfoot. I climbed over it.

The damage began to decline after some nine blocks. Something that looked like pavement appeared again. A couple of blackened houses were still standing. They were joined by other tottering frames. As I moved forward I began to have the creepy feeling that I was being watched. I whirled around, saw movement behind a broken window. A slice of white face, a flash of long red hair. Both face and hair were gone by the time I got closer.

Up ahead a shadow slid across a charred brick wall. I put on a burst of speed. A black-haired figure that could have been either a man or woman scurried around a corner, ran into one of the ruined houses.

I let the figure go. I wasn't up to a game of hide-and-seek just now. Given the language problem, I wasn't sure what I'd do with an uncooperative native even if I got hold of one.

I shrugged and walked on. I'd just about given up all hope of finding something or someone who would be of the least help when off in the distance I saw the wall. The tall structures I'd been using as guides were somewhere far beyond it. And the wall itself was a bright, cheerful red, and seemed to be spanking new.

I broke into a run.

It was new, all right, about seventy feet tall and built to last. Only that wasn't the half of it. Noises came from the other side. I heard the rumble of machines and something that could have been voices. I hardly believed it.

"Hey!" I bawled. "Anyone home? Hello!"

No answer. Either no one heard me, or no one understood me. Or possibly the whole thing was just a mirage, a hallucination brought on by two much traipsing around under the suns. I was going to find out soon enough. There had to be a door somewhere through this wall. In both directions, I saw, solid brick curved away into the distance. I flipped a mental coin. And headed right.

I tramped along kicking up the gray dust. The sounds from the other side were growing distant, dying out. I called a couple of times in a number of lingos. No dice. I began to wonder if possibly those sounds weren't coming out of loudspeakers attached to a tape deck and all I'd find on the other side was more rubble and more crazy natives having a good laugh at my expense. That's all I needed.

I met no one on my trek, saw nothing but a shadow or two flitting around in the ruins. For my money they could go chase themselves. I had no more interest in these characters; I was more than happy to write them off as a source of help. They didn't look reliable. I wanted to get over the wall, meet up with some of the responsible types who ran this world. Provided I could find any. I wasn't laying odds.

I didn't see the gate till I was almost even with it—a

small gate, set snugly in the wall and made of some kind of dark metal.

A step brought me to it. I shot a glance over my shoulder. And stopped cold. I had collected a crowd. My trackers—about six of them—were standing upright in the ruins now, staring at me openly.

The five males were nothing to brag about. They came in different heights, but they were the standard variety of scarecrow I'd been running across in this neck of the woods. The girl was something else. She had long red hair, was about five seven, stood straight and tall. If any part of her was undernourished, I couldn't spot it. Even her clothes were in spiffy shape: a pale green blouse, knee-high yellow knickers; neither item looked as if it had been snatched from the local garbage dump.

I was glad to see someone who looked halfway normal; it was an improvement. I put up a hand to wave. The whole crew—the girl included—came alive, scattered for cover, just as if I'd aimed a gun at them. I was alone again.

That settled it—the girl was as wacky as the rest of her playmates. I didn't waste time worrying about it. I had other things on my mind.

I put my palm against the gate and felt it slowly swing open.

It was a town.

Only a couple of buildings went above five stories. Most were squat, boxlike jobs. All were a uniform and dismal gray.

I didn't let the threadbare appearance get me down. I was glad to be here. By comparison to the weed-strewn rubble I'd just left behind, this place was civilization.

I looked around. The gate was unguarded. I was standing on bare concrete pavement which stretched a good hundred yards before hitting the first row of houses. In the distance I could see a few small figures moving along crooked, narrow streets.

I trotted off to join them.

I wondered vaguely what kept the folks in the bushes out of here. I didn't waste much time worrying about it. I had my own problems.

The street I hit was lined on both sides by small gray brick-and-mortar houses. Only a couple of windows to each house. The blinds were drawn on all of them. I hurried on.

The first person I met was a middle-aged overweight woman. She was dressed in gray slacks and jacket, the same shade as the buildings.

I slowed, opened my mouth to try out a couple of words. Possibly the lady would understand one.

She didn't give me the chance.

One look was all she needed. Her eyes opened wide as though she'd just spied a crocodile crawling out of the sewer system; she let out a shriek that should have roused the whole neighborhood, but didn't, then turned on her heel and scurried up the block. For a heavyweight she made good time. I let her go. She didn't seem in the mood for small talk.

I continued my jaunt, not too cheered by this greeting; it was no better than what I'd gotten from the scarecrows. I turned a corner. Two men, both gray-clad, were halfway down the block strolling toward me. They noticed me simultaneously. They didn't hesitate. They did an about-face and sprinted away.

I glanced over my shoulder, just on the off chance that someone or something behind me was frightening these good folk. Wasted effort; I had the gray street to myself. I turned back. The two men were already gone. I shook my head. I had managed to scare three citizens witless without saying a word.

Hard to imagine what an actual question would have done.

I kept walking. My reception left something to be desired, all right. I was liking it less and less. But it was too soon to panic. Possibly I was violating some taboo, neglecting to bow when meeting a stranger, or putting the wrong expression on my face. It could have been anything. And the Chairman's mind wasn't going to set me straight. I'd have to find out for myself. I figured it shouldn't take too long if I just kept hiking. I hiked.

More gray houses came and went. I met no one else, as if the populace had been warned of my presence, told to avoid me. No vehicles roamed the streets. No trees or grass added a touch of color to the dull grayness. No sounds, either of work or of merriment, came from the shuttered houses. I didn't think I was going to enjoy my stay in this burg. I hoped it would be short.

After a while sounds began to reach me again; I heard voices, movement. Someone was alive out there. I put on some speed, followed the street I was on around a corner.

The street came to an abrupt end. In its place was a large square. A half-dozen shops fronted the square. One was a clothing store. Through its plate-glass window I could see a number of jackets, coats, and trousers. All were gray. Another shop sold food, a third machinery of some sort. About two dozen gray-clad denizens of both sexes were milling around outdoors. Some sold goods out of long wicker baskets, others bought. The shops, by the look of it, were getting less business than the peddlers.

Eyeing this crowd sent an idea wiggling through my skull. It was so simple and obvious a notion that I felt pretty sure it had to be wrong. So far, the only guy I'd seen not wearing the native colors was *me*. My black jumpsuit wasn't exactly made up of rainbow hues, but it wasn't gray either. Was *that* the problem? Were the locals in a tizzy because I was out of uniform? I was about to find out.

I marched out into the square.

Whatever commerce was going on ended right there. All heads turned toward me. Arms remained frozen in midgesture. Bodies, like granite sculptures, stayed fixed in place. No actor ever had a more attentive audience. At least this crowd hadn't taken to its feet and bolted; that was something. Before the usual stampede got underway, I made a megaphone of my hands and bawled: "Listen, I'm an offworlder. I mean no harm. I've been stranded on your world. I'm with the Galactic Arm, a council member. I need help!"

I'd tried out my words in three languages—including Intergalactic—and was getting set to uncork a fourth when my audience came alive.

The women took off without a backward glance. Two of the men had more gumption. One—a large burly guy—ran within ten feet of me, bellowed something I couldn't make head or tail of, whirled around, and ran after the ladies. The other guy, a short, beak-nosed man, shook his finger at me from across the square and let loose a tirade of words, none of which made the least sense to me. By the time he was done, the pair of us had the square to ourselves. The little guy took one glance around, stopped his chatter, and beat it into the food shop. If the door wasn't locked yet, it would be by the time I reached it.

I was alone again, a condition I was rapidly getting used to and hating.

One thing was certain: I was never going to have that heart-to-heart chat I wanted with these folks even if they stopped being so skittish—not unless I dug up a translator somewhere. A hundred tongues in my noodle and I had to pick a planet that didn't speak a single one of them!

I gave the square my full attention. Not much to see, just a bunch of small, shoddy houses and a few dinky shops. The place had "provincial" written all over it. No two ways about it; I'd hit a backwater hamlet and was reaping the rewards.

I looked around for some kind of vehicle, one that I could borrow to get me out of here and over to someplace more reasonable. Nothing doing. The locals apparently hoofed it.

I sighed. Far off in the distance, still half obscured by mist or fog, were the tall buildings I'd first glimpsed from the ruined street near the weed garden. They didn't look any closer. The prospect of reaching them on foot, across who knew what terrain, did nothing to raise my spirits.

I went over to the food shop, tried the doorknob. Locked. Peering through the plate glass, I saw no one. I stepped back, raised my foot, and kicked in the door.

The little man stepped out of a back room, something that looked like a double-barreled shotgun in his hands.

I didn't bother making any speeches this time, and neither did he. I dived behind the counter as both barrels opened up. Glass shattered. The walls seemed to shake. By then I'd dug my nerve gun out of its pocket. My thumb pressed down the "wide" stud. I aimed the nozzle over the countertop, squeezed the trigger.

White light exploded.

A heavy object hit the floor: the beak-nosed proprietor.

I got to my feet. The little guy lay stretched out on

the floor. I didn't bother inspecting the damage—the charge had been on low; he'd live.

I looked through the shattered window. The square was still deserted. If anyone was around to hear the ruckus, he was minding his own business.

I emptied a small sack of grain on the floor, took what looked to be the most eatable stuff off the shelves and out of bins and baskets, and stuffed it into my sack. I tossed in a couple of bottles that seemed to have something drinkable in them. I left the storekeep to his dreams, went back outdoors, slung the sack over my back, faced in the direction of the tall buildings, and started hiking again. It was sure turning out to be a rotten day.

CHAPTER

3

Block stepped off the transmitter platform, activated the force lock which would guard the transmitter in his absence.

He looked around.

He was in an old house—wood and shingles—stuck far out in the country. Cobwebs decorated three corners of the wall. Springs jutted out of the beat-up sofa. The only chair lay on its side, two legs missing.

Block grinned. It was old home week. He was glad to be back.

The front door, he knew, was locked tight. He made his way over cracked floorboards, down a moldering hallway. The window was still open, the shutter he'd removed on the floor.

Block climbed through the window and was outside.

He took a deep breath. The sky was still black, daylight more than a few hours away.

He followed the path through the woods, the moon guiding him. He passed a shallow stream surrounded by lush shrubbery and hit the open fields. The highway was beyond.

He'd come this way before, just after the change. Only one week ago.

He wondered how much of the old Ross Block was left now.

The taxi pulled away from the curb.

Block had hitched a ride to the nearest town, caught a train in to Grand Central, rode a taxi over to the Bowery.

He stood in front of the four-story brick building that was the Men's Shelter. Three-thirty in the afternoon. A couple of bums leaned against the wall; another lay stretched out on the pavement, either dead or drunk. The entire area—tenements, run-down stores, weeds, and junk-strewn vacant lots—had a washed-out, faded look to them as though time had abandoned this place, left it to wither like a rootless tree. Even the streetlamps appeared feeble.

Block went in through the wide wooden door, ignoring the outstretched palm and pleading eyes of the derelict who'd stumbled over for a handout. A week of infighting on the Control World had made him tough.

The smell of Lysol, sweat, and urine washed over him, and even the Chairman's mind and all it contained couldn't keep him from wanting to turn and run.

His legs carried him down the hall. He turned a corner. The Big Room was deserted; the worn plastic chairs had the place to themselves. Evening would bring the bums crowding in to huddle against the night. Now only their odor remained. Block shuddered. He went back to the corridor, turned left. Block found him in his two-by-four cubbyhole—a skinny little man, maybe five three, somewhere in his sixties, dressed in a yellow T-shirt and baggy gray pants. His bald head rested on a small worn table. The shelter's floorsweep and general handyman was asleep.

Block put a hand on his shoulder. "Knobby."

The pale eyes came open; the little man sat up, blinked. "Mr. Block."

"Hiya, Knobby."

Knobby rose to his feet; Block took his hand, shook it.

"Good to see you again, Knobby," he said.

"You too, Mr. Block."

For a couple of months when his mind had been a jumble, when he hadn't known whether he was coming or going, this place had become his second home. And Knobby his only friend.

They stepped out into the hallway, ambled toward the Big Room.

"Everything okay, Knobby?"

"Couldn't be better, Mr. Block."

"Those two guys, Knobby."

"The ones you left? I called the police like you said."

"And?"

"They showed up, all right. Took them a while, though."

"How long?"

"Half hour, maybe."

"Slow."

"Not for here, Mr. Block. The Bowery ain't Park Avenue. No one cares much."

"Our two pals still peaceful?"

"Yes, sir, sleeping like babies. You sure put them away, Mr. Block. What did you hit them with?"

Block saw them again in his mind's eye: Pabst, the Chairman's adviser from the Control World—tall, thin, flat-nosed—going under the name of Charles Hastings, quietly setting Earth up for the big takeover; and his stooge, the jutting-chinned redhead. They'd both had guns, cornered him in the Men's Shelter basements. He was slated for the morgue. But he'd had a couple of the Chairman's little toys with him, a pair of memory spheres. They gave off a white piercing light. And if you weren't used to it, hadn't gone up against it a good many times before, the glowing lights put you under, sent you traipsing off to cloud nine. Block had uncorked the spheres and saved his life.

"I surprised them, Knobby."

"You sure did, Mr. Block. I went down there after you left, tied them up good."

"Smart move."

"Didn't want to take any chances. Nothin' to worry about, though. Police came, tried to wake them up." Knobby shrugged a thin shoulder. "Had to call for an ambulance, carry them out on stretchers."

"Cops find their guns?"

"Sure thing. What was it, Mr. Block? A holdup? Something more personal?"

"A little of both, I guess."

They'd reached the wide door again. The one that led to the outside world. The pair halted.

"We get some trouble from time to time. The men here, Mr. Block, they're mostly at the end of their rope. But guys from outside—well-dressed men— coming in here to pull a stickup, why, that's something for the books."

"Guess it is, Knobby. You tell the cops about me?"

"Yes, sir; you said I could. Did I do right?"

Block nodded. "Uh-huh." He gave the floorsweep his hand. "I'm in the phone book, Knobby, West Seventy-ninth Street. If there's anything I can do— anytime—you let me know."

Knobby smiled. "Mighty nice of you, Mr. Block. I'll do that. You still off the booze?"

Block said he was.

"Darnedest thing I ever saw, the way you gave up the booze. Overnight, just about. Cold turkey. You ever get the *urge*?"

"Can't say I do, Knobby."
"Darnedest thing I ever saw."

The precinct house was only six blocks away. He walked it. He didn't really know what to expect. Pabst-Hastings was a respected businessman. What had the cops made of his gun, of his presence in the Men's Shelter? Maybe the redhead had a record. That might've given the cops something to think about. Maybe not. Trouble was, Block had left things hanging, gone off to the Control World and got stuck for a whole week. Nice, maybe, for him, Nick, the Galactic Arm, and all the worlds it composed, but maybe not so nice for Earth. Still, what could Pabst do now? The Chairman was gone. The stunt Pabst was trying to pull on Earth was illegal under Galactic law. There'd be no seat waiting for him on the Galactic Council if he ever got home, just a quiet cell in some penal colony.

Here on Earth, he knew, Pabst had more than a couple of options. He was president—and probably chief stockholder—of what was by all accounts a booming business. He could carry on with it, be sitting pretty at least by Earth standards. Or he could keep the underground network he'd built, play the angles on that end—the illegal side. Or some combination of both. The Chairman's memory didn't help much in second-guessing Pabst. Block had the external data of his life down pat. But the rest of it, what made the ex-adviser tick, what went on inside him, that was still a puzzle. Pabst had been the Chairman's tool—a useful one—but the Chairman had never bothered getting below the surface. That, it appeared, was Block's job now. He wasn't looking forward to it. Pabst, by his own admission, had murdered at least two people who'd gotten in his way: Dr. Pavel and Anna, his daughter. And probably a whole lot of others. But Block had no evidence to prove it. And wasn't sure he wanted to. Uncovering the truth about Pabst might put a spotlight on the Galactic Arm, too, irrevocably changing the course of Earth's history. He wasn't ready for that yet. He needed time to sort things out, to reach some conclusions. He wondered if Pabst would give him that time?

The sergeant directed Block to a Detective Loufer. He found him in a small, cluttered, windowless office, a beefy man somewhere in his mid-fifties with gray hair, a wrinkled brow, and an ashtray full of cigarette butts on his desk. He wore a dull gray suit.

Block told him who he was.

"The guy from the Men's Shelter fracas?"

Block admitted it.

"You flatten those guys?"

Block gave him a yes.

"What'd you use, a double whammy?"

Block smiled. "Something like that."

"I can believe it."

"Had trouble waking them?"

"Yeah."

"How much?"

"A lot."

"What's a lot?"

"Would you believe a couple days in Bellevue?"

Block whistled. "They okay?"

"The skinny guy seemed okay, last I saw of him. The redhead still looked kind of bleary-eyed. I think he knew his name, but I wouldn't bet on it. Tell me, Mr. Block, off the record, what'd you do, slip 'em something?"

"In their booze?"

"Yeah. In their booze." The detective grinned.

Block grinned back. "Maybe. But nothing you could prove."

Loufer waved him to a wooden straight chair. Block seated himself, watched as Loufer put a match to a Winston, took a long drag.

"You're lucky, Block. Lucky those guys didn't press charges."

"*I'm* lucky."

"Damn right. Don't know what you did to 'em. But you sure as hell did *something*."

"Hold it," Block said. "Haven't you got it backward?"

"I don't think so, Mr. Block."

"Those guys had guns."

"Yeah. And permits to go with 'em. You gonna tell me, Mr. Block, that a hotshot businessman like Charles Hastings tried to stick you up in the Men's Shelter? Come on, Mr. Block, who's kidding who?"

"What about the other guy?"

"Hastings's bodyguard, Lew Jenks. You never came in to file a complaint, Mr. Block. Why?"

"Was busy."

"Sure." Detective Loufer leaned back in his chair. "Busy. Hastings clammed up, too. Said it was a *private* matter, nothing that concerned us."

"And this Jenks?"

"Jenks let Hastings do the talking for him. Jenks was kind of unsteady. Doctors wanted to keep him a couple days for observation."

"That bad, eh?"

"Worse. Some talk about brain damage, Mr. Block. But Hastings wouldn't hear of it. Checked himself and Jenks out the next day. What Hastings says is gospel for Jenks, at least in his current state. Doc let him go. And we let 'em both go too. Nothing to hold 'em on."

"Nothing."

"Yeah. You maybe would've been a different story. Assault."

"Jenks, I suppose."

"Didn't look too hot to me, Mr. Block. Looked kinda beat up."

"He'll live."

"Think so?"

"Know so."

"Lot more than we know."

Block shrugged.

Loufer said, "Wouldn't want to tell us what it's all about."

"That's right, I wouldn't."

"Private matter, like Hastings said."

"Uh-huh."

"We tried to find you, Mr. Block."

"Yes?"

"The old guy at the Men's Shelter gave us your name."

"I told him to."

"Real civic-minded of you, Mr. Block. Those two guys, Hastings and Jenks, when they didn't wake up, we went looking for you. Funny."

"What is?"

"Couldn't find you."

Block leaned back in his chair, folded his arms in his lap. Through the partially open door he could hear voices, shuffling feet, typewriters clicking away, the hustle and bustle of a Manhattan police station. He looked around at the pale yellow walls of Loufer's office, the pair of naked lightbulbs that glowed weakly from the ceiling, and at the tired man who sat staring at him from across his littered desk. Block almost regretted coming here. As a welcoming party it was a bust. He was feeling more like the suspect and less like the victim by the minute.

"Is that so?" Block said.

"Yeah. Not because we didn't try. Only some half-dozen R. Blocks in the phone book. A couple more in Queens, Brooklyn. None in the Bronx."

"And only two of those in the city are Ross."

"That's right. You didn't turn out to be the undertaker. So that made you the guy on West Seventy-ninth Street. Maybe. We sent a guy around to check."

"Bet you didn't find out much."

"Oh, a little. Got your description from the super; called your landlord, found out your rent was paid up in advance for a couple of years."

"Through the bank," Block said. "Phone and utilities, too. It's a service."

Loufer nodded. "Found out you hadn't been around in a stone's age. Neighbors almost forgot what you looked like. Same for the super."

"How is Gus?"

"Fine. We got your business address from the landlord."

"Old Mr. Rice okay?"

"Just dandy. You work for the *Daily Register*. Or used to. Your boss, Mr. Cohen—he's fine too, Mr. Block—says you upped and vanished about a year ago. Just skipped out, it seems."

Block grinned at the detective. "That's not a crime, is it?".

Loufer shook his head. "Nope. But you sure scared the shit out of some people. We had a missing persons out on you."

"I'm found now," Block said.

"Looks that way. But you sure raised a ruckus for a while. Your boss had us beating the bushes something fierce."

"Ben's a worrier."

"Had good reason. You were working on some story about the rackets."

"Yes."

"Any luck?"

"A little."

"Want to talk about it?"

"Uh-uh."

"I suppose the *Register* gets first crack?"

"Right."

"I'll watch for it, Mr. Block."

"Sure," Block said.

"Didn't tell your girlfriend you were going undercover either, did you?"

"You guys do quite a job."

He shrugged. "It's all in the files. She came to us—Nora Clifford. Along with your boss. Would you believe they were *very* upset?"

"Nora knows I'm back."

"Good."

"Anything else?" Block asked.

"That's about it, Mr. Block."

He rose to go.

"You'll be at your Seventy-ninth Street address?"

"Uh-huh."

"We may want to speak with you again."

"Sure."

"Mr. Block."

"Yes."

"Try not to get lost this time."

"I'll try."

"Thanks."

Block nodded, left the stationhouse; he was glad to go.

CHAPTER
4

I said bye-bye to the square, passed more shuttered houses, more dead streets. The gray pavement wound its way crookedly through the gray town. Less than six hours ago I'd been on top of the universe. Now I was somewhere near the bottom. The cranky denizens of this burg had a fit whenever you looked at them. Their lingo was a nightmare. And everything I'd seen so far could have come smack out of an old Earth Sears, Roebuck catalogue way back when. Just great. Talk about primitive. With that kind of technology it shouldn't take more than a couple of lifetimes before I got off this damn world. If I was lucky.

The gray houses and streets fell behind me.

I trudged on. Hours seemed to slip by. I kept moving.

After a while I hit another stretch of civilization: more streets and houses. They had the ramshackle look of the wasted area I'd first bumped into. No one came out to greet me. The pavement was busted up plenty. Soon it turned to dirt.

I stood still, breathing hard, and listened. A wind

was rising; it cooled the sweat on my forehead. Otherwise, nothing, no sound of life or people.

I plunked down on a handy cinder block that was lying in midroad, fished around in my sack for something to chew on, came up with two round objects—one green, the other yellow—that might've been fruit. I ate both. They weren't bad. They weren't good either.

I finished off my snack with a swig of the bottled stuff. It burned a wide streak down my middle. I liked that. Good to know the locals weren't hooked on prohibition—especially if I was going to become one of 'em. I took a couple more swigs and recorked the jug. I didn't want to get too happy—not without good reason.

I got to my feet, squinted at the still-distant tall buildings, slung the pack over my back, and continued my trek.

I didn't get very far.

The joy juice that'd been bubbling around inside me went flat without notice. And died.

I reeled backward, almost dropping my sack, as wave after wave of fear crashed over me.

I seemed to be caught in a whirlpool, the ground spinning around me.

I didn't have to think twice about what was happening. *I knew*. Time to cash in your chips, Siscoe, I thought to myself. The damn grub's done you in. Not meant for tourists, just locals. Here one day, gone the next. Those were the breaks.

Something like a mule kicked me in the noodle. I sat down hard on the ground, which seemed to tilt. I fell over sideways. What a way to go, I thought; I'd lived through gang wars back on Earth, hand-to-hand combat, and even the hoosegow, and now I was going to be bumped off by a piece of fruit! I was sweating plenty. Any second I expected to be handed my halo, harp, and wings. Or more likely a pitchfork.

Another wave of fear beat down on me. And with it came an image in my noodle.

At first it was blurred, fuzzy, as if a picture tube had gone on the blink. Then it began to take shape. I was taking a gander at the tall buildings I'd been seeing, but from up close. The place seemed lively enough. There were folks walking the streets, and only a couple of them wore gray. Some of the buildings seemed pretty tall—possibly over twenty stories—and they weren't all the same color. An occasional vehicle scooted along too.

Not bad for a delusion, but hardly the type I'd order just before swinging through the pearly gates.

Buildings, people, and cars vanished. Other images took their place. A garage door slid open. Men on cycles rolled up a ramp, rode through the doorway, and wheeled off up the street. Their cycles made plenty of racket. The men grim-faced, goggled, and in full blue uniforms. They wore holsters on their belts, and long-nosed weapons were slung over their shoulders. This bunch didn't look as if they were just kidding around.

The image faded.

I tried to sit up. It took a while, but I did it. Now if I could only get to my feet I'd be showing real progress. I decided to rest up a bit before making this final effort. Big doings take lots of planning.

Meanwhile the scenery was still whizzing around me. Only I wasn't so worried anymore. The hijinx in my bean had cheered me. There was just a chance I was going to come out of this okay, that the stuff I'd swallowed wasn't fatal. Merely something that loused up the brain and nervous system. I could live with that. *I hoped*.

I put both palms flat against the ground, was all set to shove, when the show in my noggin heated up again. I postponed the main event—standing up—and gave this latest illusion my full attention; it was a doozy.

The men on cycles were on a wide highway now. To their right and left purplish fields stretched toward a horizon that lost itself in grayish mist. The tall buildings were behind the riders, growing smaller. The same buildings I was seeing now, only from a slightly different angle.

The roadway took a turn and the angle righted itself: sight and image became one. How about that?

I took a closer peep at the riders. Their new surroundings hadn't done much to improve their disposition; they seemed just as mean-faced as before.

I grinned at what my brain, helped along by a bit of rotten chow, had cooked up. The image was clear as day. The lead rider, a tall, wiry guy, with a string of ribbons and medals along his chest, even had a mole on his left cheek; his nose was crooked and he'd nicked himself while shaving.

I had to hand it to myself. I'd more imagination than I'd figured.

The image vanished.

This seemed like a swell time to try getting up before another hallucination took a swipe at me.

I climbed to my feet slowly, not sure they would hold me. I stood very still and took a deep breath. So far, so good.

I took a step. And the damn visions popped back into my skull.

The cycle guys had made some progress since last I'd seen them. The purple fields were gone. In their place were battered houses, broken roadways, wild shrubbery.

The tall buildings were there too, almost the same size I was actually seeing then, just a mite bigger.

A notion began to circulate through my cranium:

When the guys with the guns finally reached here, the buildings I saw through my eyes and those I imagined would be *exactly* the same size.

I almost grinned, but not quite. A vague uneasiness plucked at me. The street I was on ran for a few blocks, then curved out of sight. Was the highway in my mind's eye behind it? Were a bunch of goons *really* heading my way?

The idea was too nutty. The junk I'd eaten was putting some cock-eyed thoughts in my noodle.

On cue the hallucination reared up again. It began with the riders, their cycles kicking up dust as they hit a stretch of dirt roadway.

The angle shifted.

I had a bird's-eye view of the gang. I was gazing down from some great height. They were small, distant, no larger than bugs. They seemed to crawl along a narrow black ribbon which curved its way through toy townlets, small patches of purple which were fields, over and around rises that looked no bigger than ant hills.

I shook my head trying to clear it. No dice. If anything the vision grew stronger, blotting out the gutted houses and craggy terrain around me.

I was diving down toward the highway. The riders were left far behind; I had another goal, it seemed.

I skimmed over the road following its crooked path across the landscape. I didn't have all that far to go. The first beat-up houses I spotted told me where this was. Either the ruined hamlet I was camping in, or its blood brother.

I turned a couple of corners, passed some brick piles which had once been homes, and came to the most familiar sight of all: *me*.

The me in my mind's eye had on a black jumpsuit, was standing on a street full of crumbling houses, busted streets. We looked at each other. The me had a quizzical expression on his face. He pointed over his shoulder up the road.

Somewhere up that road, I knew, were the blue boys.

The me stood there, smack in the middle of my mind. He shook his head at me, an expression of pure disgust on his face. Then he bowed once. And vanished.

I wasn't feeling any too hot. The poison-grub theory was dandy and even fit the facts. But something was wrong with it. I had an okay imagination, and doped chow might have given it a boost. But not this much of a boost.

Someone was trying to tell me something. And because I couldn't take a hint I had all but run out of time.

I was ready and eager to take a hint now.

I stood waiting. The wind brought me odors I couldn't place, raised a ruckus that covered any far-off sounds. I was starting to get jumpy.

Well? I thought.

Instantly, I was rewarded for my one word. An image snapped into my think-tank.

He was short, skinny, almost bald, with large nose and ears and a pointy chin. He looked to be somewhere in his early sixties. He wore green slacks, a yellow short-sleeved shirt. And was grinning from ear to ear. He bowed, like the Siscoe image of a second ago. There was only empty space around him, then a road appeared under his feet. On it, in the distance, came the riders—sure, that figured.

What do I do? I thought at him.

The broken houses sprang up in my head. I saw myself heading for one on the double, watched as I hurried through a lopsided doorway, hid behind a crumbling wall.

I didn't have to be told twice.

I hotfooted it over to one of the larger brick houses

just off the road. The roof and top floor were mostly gone. That left two other stories. The walls seemed okay, didn't look as though they might topple over on me.

The lopsided door hung on only one hinge. I opened it very carefully, stepped through, and closed it behind me. I had disturbed nothing, left no tracks. My hiding place ought to be safe enough.

I chose a nice spot by the window, sat down to wait.

When's the show supposed to begin? I thought at the little man.

I waited for an answer, but got none. My mind was my own again. I began to wonder if maybe I *was* crazy.

My experience with telepaths was a bit limited. Except for Ganz, I hadn't known any. But as far as I could tell, I'd been contacted by the real McCoy. Ganz had used words and the little guy—if that's who this was—pictures. But the results were the same: I'd gotten the message. That much I knew. What I couldn't figure was *why* I'd been tipped off in the first place, or how the little guy even knew I existed. The pair of whys bothered me. Along with my informant's reliability. Were the blue boys really going to swoop down on me, or was I playing hide-and-seek with no one but myself in the game?

I peered over the windowsill. I had a pretty good view of the road. There was nothing on it.

I began to fidget, a not too pleasant thought wiggling through my bean: Maybe I was being set up; possibly my lying low here, my staying put in one spot, would only aid the opposition, make it simpler for them to nab me.

By now I was feeling like myself again. The anxiety and weakness were gone, a by-product not of the chow, but more likely the little guy's poking around in my noodle. Just possibly it was time to beat it, get moving again and take my chances.

I decided to sit on the idea for a while longer, just in case the little guy was on the up-and-up.

I was glad I did.

First I heard them—a distant purr of engines, which grew to a roar as they got closer. Then I got an eyeful.

In my mind I had seen close to a dozen riders. My mind had been a piker. A whole troop was more like it. All the riders carried hardware, some as many as three guns apiece. They didn't look like the rescue squad. They looked more like the boys who handled the executions. I eased down on the floor—well out of sight—till this bunch scooted by.

I didn't kid myself; they'd be back—it was just a matter of time. They'd hit Grayburg—where someone must've sounded the alarm—and find out I'd scrammed. Some good citizen would point down the road and the blue boys would be off and running. Along with me.

Time to make myself scarce. I wondered how and where. I didn't have long to wait for an answer. An image formed in my brain. The little guy was back. This time in a black jumpsuit. Mine. The little guy was a smartass. Then I was there too, standing next to him. A building took shape around the pair of us—the one I was in. The little guy melted out of the picture, leaving me. I watched myself go to the front door, open it, and step outside. I didn't go back to the roadway, but went behind the house and struck out across the fields. Soon I was walking through shoulder-high stalks with giant purple leaves growing out of them. I was heading north away from the house. I went on this way, very fast as in a dream, for what looked like a good long time, if not quite forever. I reached the end of the field. I kept going over a flat plain covered by short yellowish grass or weeds. I came to a lake. I took off boots, rolled up my pants, and waded into the water. The lake was shallow. I walked across it in jig time. Trees were on all sides of me. I worked my way through them. A small village was at the other end of the forest stretching for no more than three blocks. The houses seemed to be in good shape, but the place seemed deserted. The sky got dark, and I knew it was nighttime. I chose a house. The door was unlocked. Inside, I found the bedroom, stretched out on the wide, soft bed, and went to sleep.

The image faded.

That's it? I threw a thought at the little guy.

Nothing.

Still there? I asked.

More nothing.

I stood by the window and thought it over.

The scenario the little guy had provided left something to be desired. It didn't say who he was, what he wanted, didn't tell me why the blue boys were after my hide.

And the trip he'd mapped for me didn't look like a picnic.

On the other hand, shooting it out with the blue boys looked even less inviting. And what chance did I have going off on my own, trying to outsmart the opposition on its own turf? My best bet—obviously—lay in following the little guy's advice. I didn't like it one bit. But then, I hadn't liked anything since hitting this world.

CHAPTER

5

Block used a corner pay phone, fed it a dime, dialed Nora's number. She answered on the second ring.

"It's me, honey."

"Ross?"

"Uh-huh."

"Thank goodness!"

"Easy does it."

"Ross."

"Yes?"

"It's a week."

"I know."

"A *whole* week."

"I'm okay, Nora."

"Are you?"

"Yes."

"I didn't know what to think."

"I'm sorry, sweetie."

"I thought you'd had a relapse."

"Uh-uh."

"Or something even worse."

"I got tied up."

"Tied up?"

"I remember who I was, Nora, what'd happened."

"All of it?"

"Uh-huh."

"No blank spots?"

"None."

"Oh, sweetheart, I'm so happy for you, so glad."

"Don't mind much myself," Block said.

"But you didn't call."

"I couldn't."

"*Why*? I thought you were dead, Ross. I was sure they'd killed you."

"They almost did."

"Oh, Ross."

"Almost wasn't good enough. I'm alive and kicking, honey."

"You could have called somehow."

"Listen. Remember the corpse they fished out of the drink?"

"I'll never forget."

"Well, I was right."

"Right?"

"It was Nash."

"And?"

"I found out who killed him."

"Oh, Ross."

"And they found out I knew."

"Darling—"

"It was touch and go for a while. I couldn't call, believe me."

"Ross."

"Yes?"

"Is it over?"

He took a deep breath. "It's still going on, honey."

"God."

"Not to worry."

"How *can* you say that?"

"Listen. It's a standoff."

"What?"

"I can't prove they killed Nash. They know that. They're not coming after me. That's the important thing. And maybe I won't go after them either."

"*Maybe?*"

"I don't know yet."

"You *want* them to kill you?"

"No one's killing anyone."

"They killed this Nash. You just said so."

"That was then."

"*Then?*"

"Uh-huh."

"I don't understand a word you're saying, Ross."

"It's simple."

"Simple."

"Yes."

"Tell me."

"I've got too much on them now."

"Meaning what?"

"Anything happens to me, their racket gets blown sky-high."

"You're crazy, Ross."

"Uh-uh. I've got them where I want them."

"Ross."

"Yes."

"You're a *reporter*."

"So?"

"Not a one-man police force."

"Listen. There are things I can't tell you, Nora."

"And you've been sick."

"I'm much better, honey."

"You don't sound better."

"I've even put on weight."

"In a week?"

"Clean living."

"What you sound like, Ross, is weird."

"Come on, Nora."

"Single-handed, you're going after this ... this racket."

"Maybe not."

"One racket more, one mob less, what does it matter, Ross?"

"It matters."

"It *doesn't*. Not to you. Not to me. Maybe not to anyone."

"You don't understand, honey."

"I understand. This is some personal vendetta."

"It's not."

"What are you trying to prove, Ross?"

"Nothing. It's just something I've got to finish, that's all."

"They'll finish *you*."

"I'm not in danger."

"How would you know? Did this Marty Nash think he was in danger? Didn't he have something on the mob too?"

Marty Nash swam before Block's eyes. Not the kid he'd known in grade school, but the carcass lying on a slab in the morgue, its head chopped off, the hands severed from the bony wrists, the neat, round hole under its heart. Nash had died because he'd known too much, and Pabst's men had made sure he wouldn't be able to tell anyone what he knew. And tracking down the truth behind Nash's death was what had gotten Block involved in this whole mess to begin with. He shuddered. The Chairman's mind gave him an edge. But it had certain limitations. It couldn't stop knives or bullets, couldn't dodge an oncoming car, or deflect a cinder block tossed from some rooftop. The Chairman's mind was only a tool, not a shield against violence. He was as vulnerable as the next guy. More so because he was planning to take on the Pabst outfit. Maybe the Chairman's ex-adviser would listen to reason, maybe Block could offer him some kind of deal, a return to the Control World. Maybe a seat on the Council. Pabst, as far as Block knew, was no worse than the average Galactic statesman. Their crimes—thousands of them—were all catalogued in the Chairman's mind. And the Chairman himself was the worst of the lot. He'd talk to Pabst, lay it on the line. But somehow he wasn't all that confident Pabst would listen. Being privy to the Chairman's mind had made Block a cynic.

He said, "Nora, I'm going to be *very* careful."

"When will I see you, Ross?"

"Soon."

"When soon?"

"I don't know."

"Ross."

"I'm not sure how to handle this yet, you understand? It may be over, done with, before we know it."

"Darling—"

"I want you to trust me, Nora."

"And I want to see you. *Now.*"

"I can't."

"Why not?"

"I don't want you mixed up in this."

"No danger. You said so."

"Let's not take chances, Nora."

"But *you're* taking chances."

"That's me."

"Oh, Ross, this is so stupid."

"Listen. I remember who I am, I know what I'm doing. Maybe it doesn't sound that way, but I do. A couple of breaks and I'll wrap this thing up. That'll be that. We'll have lots of time, Nora. Believe me. There's nothing stupid about this."

"Oh, Ross."

"I've got to go now."

"You'll call me?"

"Soon."

"Promise?"

"Uh-huh."

"I miss you."

"Same here."

"Be careful."

"I will."

He hung up the receiver, turned, walked down the street. Only a stroll to SoHo. He could drop in on Nora, call time out on wrangling with Pabst, go back to being the simple guy he used to be, with only one set of memories bobbing around in his brain, and only one little world to worry about. He wouldn't mind. All. this knowledge had come too quickly for comfort. He needed time to digest it, to figure out where Ross Block began and the Chairman's mind left off.

Only he didn't have time.

He had to move in on Pabst fast, before whatever he was up to got too big to stop. If it wasn't already.

Block turned west. Soon he was hurrying past small brownstones and an occasional tall white brick apartment house. More than a dozen trees lined each block. The air was relatively clean, given the number of cars that rolled by. There were even birds. He looked them over as though seeing them for the first time.

He wasn't sure what to make of it all, how to judge it. No chance on the Control World for any sightseeing. But his mind was full of sights and sounds which had once belonged to the Chairman and maybe some sixty other guys whose tapes he'd been fed.

It was confusing as hell. Block put up his hand and hailed a taxi.

He got off in front of a large familiar twenty-story building. He ran his eyes up and down the yellow brick facade and saw no changes. The only change was in him.

He rode the self-service elevator up to the twelfth floor. He was lucky and met no one. Block was in no mood to exchange greetings with neighbors, to explain his long absence.

He padded down the carpeted hallway, stopped before 12C, fumbled with the keys he'd gotten from Nora a week ago, turned them in the lock, slid open the door, and stepped inside.

His back to the door, Block stood and took in the floor-to-ceiling bookcases, thick green-and-orange carpet, hi-fi set and speakers, color Sony, the racks of tapes and records, lamps and stands, chairs, sofa, and dark blue drapes. It all washed over him. He took a deep breath and the familiar odors of home— dust-covered and a bit musty now—filled his nostrils. He felt his knees go weak. Almost a full year since he'd been here last. Pabst and his goons had put him through the wringer. He'd lost his memory for a while and wandered around the Bowery, a certified bum. And to top things off, Pabst and his redhead pal—this Jenks—had tried to kill him. He wondered how easy it would be to let bygones be bygones. Maybe not so easy, after all.

Block had a five-room apartment, and he wandered through each of the rooms, marveling at them, as though he'd just unexpectedly come across long-lost friends. In a way he had. He was a reporter again back on the *Register*, waiting for his big break. The break had come, of course, but from an unexpected source. Nothing, but nothing, would ever be the same again. And Block wasn't sure he liked the change.

After a while he called it quits and got busy. He stripped off his clothes, climbed into a fresh blue sport shirt, a rust tweed jacket, and brown slacks. He looked respectable. He fished some loose bills out of a cookie jar, got his press card out of the briefcase, and slipped these items into his wallet. He'd borrowed a laser from the Control World. He stuck it into a pants pocket. Block gave himself the once-over in the mirror. Not bad. Food on the Control World had fattened him up. He stood a straight five nine, weighed in at about a hundred and sixty, and was a long way from looking like something the dog had dug up in the backyard.

He couldn't ask for more. He turned and headed for the front door.

Ross Block was as ready as he'd ever be.

CHAPTER
6

I was right—the trip was no picnic.

I left my hiding place on the double before the blue boys came back for another look-see and beat it across the fields.

That part of the operation went off without a hitch. The brown grass—or whatever it was—was only a couple of inches tall, and the ground was reasonably firm under it. I moved along at an okay clip.

After that things weren't so easy.

Getting through the giant stalks with their large purple leaves had looked like a snap when I was just slogging through my mind. My on-the-site experience was something else. The little guy in the black jumpsuit had neglected to tell me that the leaves cut like razors and the stalks were about as pliable as lead pipes. The jaunt took a while. By the time it was over I was ready to sack out then and there.

No such luck.

The plain of yellow weeds seemed to stretch for miles. The ground here was soft and mushy; I sank in up to my ankles with each step I took.

By the time I hit the lake it was already dusk and I could barely see the trees on the other side. I took off my boots, rolled my pants up to the knees, stepped in, and promptly sank up to my waist. I made it across the water swimming the last third of the way.

I was cursing the little guy plenty as I stumbled around the forest—wet, chilled and bone-tired—probably going in circles; as a travel agent he was a bust.

I'd all but tossed in the sponge, given up hope of ever hitting the village, and was hunting for a nice hole in the ground to bed down in, when I heard the sounds.

I stood still, tried to keep my teeth from chattering, and cocked an ear. The wind was still blowing, rustling the leaves. I waited for things to quiet down. In a momentary lull I heard the sounds again: voices. There shouldn't've been any voices within miles—at least not according to my trusty guide; it looked as though the little jerk had laid another egg. Or maybe the blue boys had gotten wind of my itinerary and were sitting around waiting for me to walk into their arms. Either way I didn't like it.

I had two choices now, neither of them too hot. I could let the voices be, head off in another direction, and hope it led somewhere sensible, or I could sneak up on the voices and see what they were up to. I didn't know what I'd gain by the latter course, but it seemed smarter than just taking it on the lam again. And maybe easier too. I went toward the voices.

It took a bit of doing. The wind tossed the voices around in one direction, then another; in between they vanished altogether. I couldn't use the small pocket flash that came with the jumpsuit, not unless I wanted to attract attention. I felt my way along, stepping around trees. After a while I saw a light.

That made things smoother. I had a definite goal now. I moved slowly, carefully, trying very hard not to make a sound.

I saw dark, square shapes which became houses as

I got closer. The light was a small flickering campfire that someone had started in what looked to be a backyard. Three figures sat around it. They weren't blue boys.

I crept up on them, moving from tree to tree, till there were no more trees, just a small clearing, and then houses.

The three figures were all male. I couldn't tell their ages. They didn't look especially undernourished, but their clothes were nothing to brag about, and they had scraggly beards and longish, unkempt hair.

The last time I'd tried to hobnob with some of the locals, the results had been far from satisfactory. But these babies were a different sort, neither gray townsfolk nor tattered scarecrows. Possibly they'd hold still for a bit of communication.

If nothing else I could use the fire to dry off my duds.

I stepped out of the woods and into the clearing. The three guys—who looked discouragingly like earth hobos—didn't notice me. I moved silently in their direction. I sneezed. Not exactly the way I'd intended to introduce myself, but it got their attention. The three of them jumped up as though I'd set off a firecracker under their noses. Their heads turned toward me in unison; they stared. They looked ready to run for their lives at the drop of a hat.

I held up my hand, put a friendly smile on my face. It hadn't worked before on this world, but you could never tell. I took a cautious step toward them. By now my smile had grown to a broad grin which felt as if it had been pasted on to my kisser permanently. I wagged my head in an idiot's parody of delight. Anything to keep these birds from taking a powder.

I needn't have bothered.

Like statues come to life, the three unfroze. One

reached behind him, and a long-bladed knife appeared in his hand. He leered at me, took a step forward. The guy next to him bent over, scooped up a heavy branch, his eyes never leaving mine. I saw he was drooling from the side of his mouth. The last of these beauties flexed his fingers; he didn't need a weapon, his hands were good enough to do the job.

They advanced slowly, jabbering and crooning at me as though the meaningless words they were sending my way might keep me from bolting.

My smile went the way of the dodo. Disgust took its place. What was wrong with the natives on this world? Were they *all* bananas?

I reached into my pocket; my hand came up holding the nerve gun. I grinned and nodded goodnaturedly as I gave them the full charge.

The three creeps lay stretched out peacefully on the ground. In about twelve hours they'd return from cloud nine, if exposure didn't get them first. I wasn't going to worry about it.

I stepped over their inert bodies, went to the fire, and slowly sank to the ground. My trip through the wilds had left me sore and aching. I could feel muscles I didn't even know I had. At least I was still in one piece. For now.

The flames started to bake me. I liked that. The plasto fibers of my jumpsuit began to dry out pronto. I sighed, reached into my trusty sack, and helped myself to dinner. If nothing else, all this exercise had worked up an appetite. The chow didn't taste half bad. It still wasn't all good. But what was? I took another snort out of the bottle. No little man popped up in my noodle.

You with me, pal? I shot him a thought.

A lot of silence filled my cranium. Just as well. I'd had enough fun for one day.

The fire was growing low, the night air chill. I didn't feel like hauling branches all night to feed the flames. The little guy's game plan had me napping in one of the houses. It didn't seem like such a bad idea.

I got to my feet stiffly, stretched, went over to my three natives, kicked one in the ribs: still out for the count. Satisfied that my nerve gun had done its job, I trotted off for the nearest house.

The door opened on squeaky, rusted hinges; the sound gave me the willies. I dug my pocket flash out of its pouch, shone the light around.

The little chump who'd been sending me brain waves had pictured this house as a model domicile. Some gag. There were cracks in the floor, walls, and ceiling; the furniture—what litte there was of it—was all busted up; and the place smelled as if it had been used as a sewer in its spare time. Beady eyes glared out at me from under the wreckage. I didn't hang around to find out what they were. I now knew why the three stooges had decided to camp outdoors. I hurried to join them.

I had a choice. I could build up the fire and spend a cozy night huddled next to it, a sitting duck for anyone who happened to come along. Or I could go hide in back of a house and freeze. It didn't take much figuring. I decided to take my chances. This place, as far as I could tell, was next to nowhere. Anyone who went to all the trouble of getting here deserved a crack at me.

I fixed the fire, used my sack for a pillow, and went to sleep, hoping the little things in the houses wouldn't come out and nibble on me.

In the dream I was running uphill, the little guy by my side. The harder we ran, the more we seemed to stay in place. That wasn't so good, because the blue boys were after us. There were about twenty of them on their motorbikes down at the base of the hill. They weren't making much time either.

I looked up and the redheaded girl—the one I'd spotted with the scarecrows—was waving to us from the top of the hill. She wasn't alone. A fat party I had never seen before stood by her side. He was about six feet tall, weighed over three hundred pounds. He had a longish head with a small dainty beard. He was urging us on too with waves of his gigantic arm. I tried to run harder, but each step drove my feet deeper into the ground. I looked around and the little guy was gone. I glanced over my shoulder. The motorbikes had risen off the ground, were flying after me. That wasn't fair at all! The blue boys had their guns out, were taking aim. I put on one final burst of speed, and sank in up to my neck.

I woke up.

It was dark, cold. The campfire had burned down, was reduced to embers. I'd slept for a good while, then. Why did I feel so uneasy? My forehead, I noted, was covered with sweat; my jumpsuit was pasted to my body as if I'd gone in for another dip in the lake.

My hand groped for the flash, found it. Light danced out across the ground. The three goons I'd blasted were still snoozing away, as motionless as the branches I'd piled for fuel. Nothing to worry about from them. But something was eating at me.

I remembered the dream.

As though a dam had busted open, wave after wave of anxiety poured over me. I almost tumbled onto my side. My mouth was open, gasping. My stomach felt as if a large boot was busy kicking it.

The last time this happened, the little guy had

popped into my mind, and the fireworks had subsided. No such luck now.

I tried to figure what was causing this hullabaloo. And remembered the dream. My anxiety drained away, left me empty as if someone had pulled the plug on my emotions.

I took a deep breath, wiped the sweat from my brow. What the hell was going on?

With the juice turned off, the anxiety dampened, the dream seemed just that—a dream.

I started to get to my feet.

A huge wave of fear and terror knocked me back to the ground.

That did it, made a believer of me. The dream it was.

I gave the thumbs-up sign in my head, hoping the little guy would understand I'd gotten his message.

Again the anxiety simmered down.

I sat there trying to put two and two together. It wasn't all that easy. Something was jamming the little guy's signals. He couldn't get through to me now, except by giving me a jolt. But he had managed to infiltrate my brain while I slept. What was he trying to tell me?

The blue boys had been chasing me on their bikes. Then they'd taken to the air.

Was I going to be strafed by an airplane? Or would I receive a more intimate visit?

I looked up at the sky, saw only blackness. I listened for sounds, heard lots of wind and nothing else.

Was I right? Or had I misread the bulletin?

I waited for some hint from my benefactor, some sign that would tell me which way to go. No soap. The station—with me as its only viewer—had left the air, the little guy off on a coffee break or something. A helluva time to be on my own again.

I sat there staring at the embers, and an idea began scooting through my noodle. It wasn't the best notion, but all I could come up with on such short notice; I hadn't planned to get stranded on this world, let alone in this ghost town.

I got busy. I started dumping more branches on the embers. I used my foot to stir things up. Soon I had a nice blaze going.

I went back to my three victims. A couple of kicks in the ribs didn't seem to disturb them at all. They'd keep till company arrived. I dragged them over to the fire.

Rummaging through a small, grimy bundle that belonged to one of these bums, I found a bottle. I unscrewed the cap, took a sniff. If the colorless and odorless liquid inside was a euphoric or intoxicant, it wasn't advertising the fact. I left it by the outstretched hand of one of my snoozers, just for effect, even if I didn't know what that effect would be.

I stood back and examined my handiwork. Not bad. The tableau would give any visitors I might have something to look at even if only for a moment. A moment was all I could reasonably expect. I hoped it would be enough.

I took my sack and retreated to the nearest house. The woods would have been a better bet, but they were too far away for what I had in mind.

I made sure there was a back door, just in case, then climbed a rickety flight of stairs to the second floor. The things in the woodwork and under the floorboards glared at me with their red, beady eyes, but stayed put. I was thankful.

I poked my head out of a second-story window. My view of hobos and campfire was unobstructed.

I settled down to wait.

If I was wrong, I'd spend what was left of the night in this chilly dump for nothing. I could stand that.

If I was right, I'd soon have company—and not just an overflight, either. With some luck maybe I'd even survive the experience.

It took the better part of an hour before I heard the hum of the first aircraft.

CHAPTER
7

Ross Block gazed at the building.

It looked innocuous enough, a twenty-three-story job of concrete and yellow brick, which had gone up some forty years ago. There were hundreds like it in midtown Manhattan. But this one, he knew, was somewhat different.

The light turned green. He crossed the street, went through the revolving door, paused briefly to inspect the building directory. Half the slots were empty, including the one Block wanted.

He stepped into a self-service elevator; his thumb pressed eighteen. He went up.

His footsteps made soft sounds on the carpeted floor as he moved toward the suite of offices at the far end of the hallway. Muffled noises from adjacent offices reached him: typing, a phone ringing, a woman's voice.

Block kept one hand stuck in his jacket pocket, his fingers wrapped around the butt of the laser.

He stopped at the door. No decal decorated its frosted-glass window. His hand went to the knob, turned it. Locked. He put his nose to the frosted glass, saw nothing through it but a blur.

Turning, he went back to the elevator, rode down to the ground floor, crossed the small lobby to a side door, opened it and started down a well-lit flight of stairs; they led to the basement.

The super was a tall heavyset man with a bald head and a large belly. He took a thick cigar from between his lips.

"McCoy, huh?"

"The export-import firm," Block said.

"Eighteenth floor?"

"Yes."

"Gone, mister."

"I know. I was just there."

"So?"

"When'd they move? Where'd they go?"

"You got business with 'em, huh?"

"Uh-huh."

"But you don't know where they went."

"That's right."

"Kind of funny, ain't it, mister?"

Block sighed, fished his wallet out of a pants pocket, handed the super a ten. "Sidesplitting," he said.

"Yeah," the super said, "McCoy pulled out a week ago last Wednesday."

"Kind of sudden, wasn't it?"

"Sudden ain't the word. Them guys had three trucks waitin' outside. Eight a.m., right on the button. Maybe twenty guys doin' the haulin'. They was out before noon. That's hustlin', huh? The boss, he told me they paid up on a three-year lease; no squawks. They just upped and went."

"Leave a forwarding address?"

"They musta *somewhere*, a big outfit like that."

"But not with you. Or anyone else in the building, I bet."

"You'd win, mister. Boss said he asked 'em. They

said forget it. That's okay with us. No skin off our nose, right?"

"Guess so. How you figure on earning that ten-spot?"

"How's about I give you the name of the movers?"

"That would do," Block said, "for a start."

"Handock. Got somethin' else, too."

"Glad to hear it," Block said honestly enough.

The super reached into the drawer of an old, battered desk, rummaged around, came up with a dog-eared address book. "Got some guys here, work for McCoy, see. Got their names, addresses, phone numbers. That oughta help some, huh?"

"Sounds good," Block said. "How come you have these names?"

"Got 'em for just about every firm in the joint. Gotta know who to call in case o' trouble, right? Fire, maybe a water pipe breakin', a burglary. Anything goes wrong, you gotta know who to call."

"That part of your job?"

"Sure, me or the front office. Whatever the boss wants."

"They got the same names you do?"

The super shrugged, stuck the cigar back in his mouth. "Maybe. Try 'em."

"I'll do that," Block said.

"You ask a lotta questions, mister."

"I sure do," Block agreed.

He jotted down the names the super had given him, exchanged so longs, and took the stairs back to the ground floor.

He used a corner phone booth to make some calls.

There was no new phone listing for McCoy—hardly a surprise. Handock gave Block all the information it had, which wasn't much. Stanford Blakely, Executive Director of Corporate Affairs at McCoy, had engaged Handock to remove all furniture from its midtown office. Blakely had paid in advance.

"Where'd you cart the stuff?" Block asked.

"Jessie Used Office Furniture. It's down in the Village."

Neither Handock nor Jessie, when Block called them, had a forwarding address for McCoy. Blakely had been their only contact, and both parties had met with him only once.

Bliss Real Estate—the managers of McCoy's building—knew no more than the others. They gave Block the same names as the super.

Block stepped out of the phone booth, turned east. His feet carried him toward Lexington Avenue. He passed a handful of small stores—a couple of groceries, a deli, a cleaners—and numerous apartment houses. The few trees he saw had lost most of their leaves. Late October. The sky was a deep, clear blue, the air crisp and clean.

He turned south on Lexington, walked to Twenty-eighth Street. Paul Draden lived in a brownstone a few houses off Lexington. Block ran his bell, was mildly surprised to find himself being buzzed into the alcove. He went up a carpeted flight of stairs. Draden—a thin, balding, middle-aged man in gray slacks, open-necked white shirt, and horn-rimmed glasses—was waiting for him by an open door on the first floor landing.

Block said, "My name's Ross Block, Mr. Draden; I'm with the *Daily Register*." He showed Draden his press card. "You were with McCoy Export-Import."

"Indeed yes, fifteen years; head clerk for twelve."

"I hope you can help me."

"Yes?"

"I'm doing a piece, Mr. Draden, on New York–based firms which've relocated recently. McCoy was one of them. But they seem to have crawled under a rug. Overnight, too."

Draden nodded. "Come in, Mr. Block, please."

Block followed him into a white-walled study, seated himself in a cushioned armchair. Draden sat on the tip of a rocker, eyed Block inquisitively.

"There's more to this than a mere business story, isn't there?"

"A little, maybe."

"I'm willing to speak with you. But it must be off the record. I can't have my name used."

"Agreed."

Draden nodded. "McCoy didn't relocate, Mr. Block, they shut their doors—permanently."

"Financial troubles?"

"McCoy was solid."

"So what happened?"

Draden shrugged. "It came out of the blue, Mr. Block. A day's notice, that's all. I still can't believe it."

"Who broke the news?"

"Mr. Blakely."

"He the big boss?"

"Next to Charles Hastings. At least in the New York office."

"Chain of command a bit muddy, I'd imagine, eh, Mr. Draden?"

"That's putting it mildly."

"You checked."

"Only out of curiosity; in my idle moments, so to speak."

"And came up with what?"

"McCoy had worldwide interests, Mr. Block; its branches were scattered across the globe. Ours was the main office, of course. But something was, shall we say, peculiar."

"Sure, let's say that."

"A number of reports crossed my desk. They were mostly quite routine in nature. But some of our overseas branches literally *never* sent in a report. At least not to my knowledge."

"Maybe they used other channels."

"They didn't."

"Checked again, eh?"

"Of course. Same holds true for some of our stateside offices. And there were names on our roster which appeared to be just that and no more."

"No people attached to them?"

"None that I could determine."

"Very curious."

Draden rocked back and forth. "Very," he agreed. "And then some."

"Do something about it?"

Draden shrugged. "None of my business, really."

"Uh-huh. Lots of businesses have a couple of hush-hush projects going from time to time, Mr. Draden, don't they?"

"Quite standard, Mr. Block."

"And you figured the McCoy goings-on for something like that?"

"I simply didn't know. I was chief clerk, not on the board of directors."

"And you noticed nothing else that was fishy?"

"I assure you, Mr. Block, I personally knew of no illegal activities the firm might be engaged in. And quite frankly, up until last Wednesday, I would have leaned over backward to give them the benefit of the doubt."

"Wednesday you got your walking papers."

"Yes."

"Kind of changed your mind then, Mr. Draden?"

Draden's jaw was firm. "No company as fiscally sound as McCoy would ever consider shutting down in such a manner, Mr. Block. It's simply not done."

"Investors take a bath?"

"They were devastated."

"Like that, eh?"

"And, moreover, they could easily have walked away with huge profits had they put their stock up for sale."

"No one bothered."

"No one."

"You looked into the matter?"

"As far as I could." Draden sighed. "It was insane."

"Anything else?"

"They left scores of deals hanging."

"Made you think, I bet."

"A company that had nothing to hide, Mr. Block, would never have done that."

"But still, Mr. Draden, you informed no one, didn't tip off the police, the SEC, the Attorney General's Office? You just sat on it?"

Draden spread his hands. "Come now Mr. Block, let us be reasonable. I had no hard evidence, merely a number of suspicions, all unverified."

"Looks pretty damning from here."

"Perhaps. But I was not McCoy's sole employee. They had hundreds. It was hardly my responsibility to initiate action."

"So you waited for someone else to blow the whistle."

"Mr. Block, the firm was *very* generous in its severance pay. Uniquely so, I should say."

"Gave everyone a bundle?"

"An entire year at full salary."

"Not bad."

"The staff was most grateful."

"I'm sure."

"And you must remember, Mr. Block, many of us who worked for McCoy still hope to remain in this field."

"Don't want to rock the boat, eh?"

"For what purpose? Those who call attention to themselves as troublemakers jeopardize their chances in the job market."

"Won't be snapped up."

"Blacklisted is more likely."

"I get the picture, Mr. Draden."

".I thought you might."

"I still need your help," Block said.

"Still off the record?"

"Uh-huh."

"What is it?"

"You were right, Mr. Draden. This is more than a business story."

"Of course."

"The *Register* has reason to believe that McCoy was pulling a number of fast ones."

"How did you come by this information, if I may ask?"

"Confidential. If we snitched on our informants, how could *you* trust us?"

"I understand."

"We'll be poking around into all aspects of the firm's operations."

"Quite a job."

"Right. I'd be grateful for as many names of employees as you can dig up."

"I have no records."

"From memory, then."

"Very well."

"Branch locations, too."

Draden nodded.

"And all you remember about the firm's business dealings."

"You don't want much, do you?"

"You'll try?"

Draden shrugged. "Why not?"

CHAPTER

8

I resisted the temptation to peek out the window. The nice, crackly fire, I knew, would draw them to me. I waited. The street below was in full view.

The thing that dropped from the sky was a round gray ball. Jets held it aloft for an instant, hovering, then it sank down some thirty yards from the fire.

Mentally I flipped through the Chairman's index file. The craft down below, by the looks of it, seemed to be an old Galactic model, long outdated, the kind you might find in a salvage lot. I wondered what the hell it was doing here. I'd figured the blue boys for cops or security forces. It hadn't occurred to me that I might be up against a local version of the Hell's Angels.

A panel slid back and four blue boys hopped out on the ground, their weapons at the ready. A moment later and a second ball swept down to join the first. Three armed uniformed guys hopped out, making it seven in the hunting party. Seven was supposed to be a lucky number; I wondered for who, me or them. I waited for more reinforcements, but there weren't any.

The troops, peering in all directions at once, began

moving toward the fire. They walked very carefully, as though expecting the ground to be mined.

They came to a halt around the fire.

My three decoys did nothing surprising; they failed to jump up and denounce me. They just lay there attracting the proper amount of attention.

One of the blue boys bent over, began to examine faces. It wouldn't take him long to figure out that none of these bearded nappers was the clean-shaven intruder they were looking for. Probably they'd try to wake the three for questioning. And when they found they couldn't, it either would or wouldn't set them to thinking. They might just go back to their gray balls and fly away. Or they could search the houses and the woods. I didn't know what they had up their sleeves, and I couldn't take the chance of finding out. There were too many of them. My nerve gun was no match for their firepower. If it came to a shootout, the odds were all in favor of the blue boys. I did something to change the odds.

I slipped my hands into the wide utility pocket of my jumpsuit, fished out the square-shaped plasto-deck igniter. It was painted a cheerful yellow and green. But there was nothing cheerful about it. Before my mishap with the transmitter, I'd been headed for the Planet of the Dead, bent on setting fire to a half-dozen tape bins. All that seemed like a couple of centuries ago. But it wasn't a full day yet. I still had the hardware to do the job.

Any second, I knew, my victims might disperse, head off in different directions. I needed them in a group.

I pressed down on the maxi stud, put duration at four seconds, and pitched the igniter out the window.

It landed in the flames.

Two of the blue boys glanced up. One even started to raise his gun.

The fire ignited, went off with a giant roar. You're not supposed to toss igniter cubes into an open fire—they explode.

I looked away from the carnage below, but only for a second.

Flame filled the street. Both blue boys and bums were lost in it. Nothing could be alive down there.

A solid sheet of flames beat against the house I was in. Some cube.

That got me moving.

The stairs all but gave under my weight. I hit the ground floor running hard. I trotted for the back door. Smoke came after me. The front part of the house was a mess. The igniter was doing its stuff with a vengeance.

Outside, I didn't slow down; I kept to the back of the houses, came out behind the pair of aircraft.

A lone blue boy was staring at the blaze, his head and shoulders sticking out of the gray craft's hatch.

If there's a crew of four in one ship, it's only reasonable to expect four more in its mate. Reason was having a field day.

The nerve gun was in my hand. I gave him the full charge. The blue boy slumped over. He was out of it. In twelve hours he'd wake up as good as new, the only one of his crew to have avoided the barbecue. Lucky blue boy.

I stood there surveying my accomplishments. Houses on both sides of the street were lighting up like matchsticks. There'd be nothing left of this hamlet in another twenty minutes. Meanwhile, the fire would be visible for miles, especially from the air. I didn't know how many gray balls were hunting for me. But if there were any hanging around this neck of the woods, I'd be having company in no time at all.

Hustling over to the craft, I dragged out its lone occupant and dumped him on the ground.

My feet found the three rungs which led up to the hatch. I reached the top, swung over the rim; a short metal ladder took me down into a padded interior with four seats.

I took the seat in front of the control panel, a logical choice.

Logic ended right there.

No window looked out at the outside world. The controls themselves seemed ordinary enough, and with a couple of lessons under my belt, I'd have been flying this crate like a pro.

Too bad no one had given me the lessons.

I hoped the Chairman had been more farsighted.

I waded through all the junk about aircraft in his mind. It didn't take more than a minute or two, although it felt like an hour.

By then I had something to go on.

No ship exactly resembled the one I was in. But a couple of antiques came close. The control panel before me began to make a sort of dim sense.

My finger pressed a round button. The viewscreen on the panel lit up and I was eyeing the outdoors in full color. Nothing had changed. The fire was doing better than ever. It had saved my neck minutes ago, but now it was a menace, a beacon pointing directly at me. If I didn't get a move on, I'd have the opposition sitting in my lap.

I turned a black knob to the right. The engine began to rumble.

My hand closed around a black lever, pulled back.

Like a giant balloon, the ship began to drift upward.

The fire below me grew smaller as I watched on the viewer, finally became a small flickering flame, as if someone had snapped on a cigarette lighter in a high wind. I expanded the viewer's range. If there were any other ships snooping about, I couldn't spot them. That meant nothing. I hunted around the panel for the electro-eye button, found it on my third try.

A small, milky green screen on the far left of the control board lit up. Four black dots were on it inching along in different directions. One of them might have been heading toward me. I didn't know. And I wasn't going to wait around to find out.

I fiddled with a couple of more levers, knobs, buttons, whatever lay under hand. When I thought I had it figured, I let my fingers do their stuff.

The craft jumped as though someone had given it a hotfoot. It moved toward the dots. I reversed order and sailed off in the other direction.

Not bad for starters. Now if I only had a destination in mind.

Not too far off in the distance I could see lights: the city, of course; the one I'd been aiming for before the blue boys had gotten in my way. Probably they'd come from there. But what difference did that make? I'd had no choice. Camping in the woods would get me nothing but a stiff neck.

I began adjusting the controls.

I could feel the night around me. I was alone in darkness except for one small moving dot on my screen. That dot—another craft—had begun heading in my direction, was closing in on me.

I dived.

I wasn't too worried. I could hold my own when it came to playing hide-and-seek in the air: I'd had some practice, had put in a good couple of hours dodging the enemy back on the penal world. The Chairman's mind was okay in a pinch, but it couldn't beat a little practical experience.

The flames behind me grew bigger, brighter. Part of the woods, I saw, had caught fire, too. The blue boys could now add firebug to the list of charges against me.

I took off across the woods, heading back the way I'd come.

The dot dropped off the screen.

I skimmed the shallow lake, swooped over the dark fields. No new dots sprang up on the viewer.

I turned my craft toward the city.

The fields flickered by below me, almost within arm's reach. As long as I hugged the ground, I figured I was safe from electro-eyes. I hugged it.

The city got closer, became more distinct. Plenty of tall buildings, lots of lights. If this was a ghost town, someone was wasting a lot of electricity.

I didn't sail right into town. I hunted up a nice clearing in a clump of woods and put the buggy down. I gave the cockpit a quick once-over, but found nothing at all. I went back to my seat, polished off the last of the chow in my sack, then broke open a new bottle and took a swig.

I climbed out of the craft, worked my way through the woods, and started hiking.

The sky turned from black to gray. I stood on a deserted street corner, the three— and four-story houses which lined both sides of the block my only company.

No fences had barred my way here, no blue boys guarded the streets. They probably had better ways to keep track of their citizens in this burg. I didn't think I'd like them.

I moved on.

An elderly woman emerged from one of the houses. She gave me a long, hard look as we passed each other—too long. But she didn't run down the block screaming. That was something.

I turned a corner and was alone again. I turned some more corners. A boy came out of a house. I hustled into a backyard, waited till he'd left, then went back to my stroll.

During the next quarter hour I hid from a short stubby guy, two little girls, and a yellow bubbletop vehicle that looked like half a grapefruit on three wheels. The place was coming alive. And I was starting to get nervous. Too much activity on the streets could ruin me.

Five minutes later I hit pay dirt.

He was a tall, youngish guy in a brown-and-gold-striped jacket and black slacks, not unlike mine. He carried a canvas bag in his right hand. He was two blocks away and heading toward me.

I flattened myself against the side of a house, waited.

A man and woman went by in the other direction. They didn't see me.

Presently the young guy stepped into view. I got a glimpse of a sharp profile, then his back was to me.

I had the nerve gun in my hand. I pressed the stud.

The guy pitched forward soundlessly.

I jumped out, caught him as he fell, and hauled him back to the side of the house.

I heard voices on the street. I didn't know if they had anything to do with me, and didn't wait around to find out.

I helped myself to the guy's jacket, left him lying there, and took off through the backyards.

Nobody chased me.

After a while I went out on the streets again. I was wearing the guy's jacket, zipped up to the collar. More people hustled along. A couple of grapefruitlike cars scooted by on the roadway. Nobody paid any attention to me. The menacing stranger in the black jumpsuit was gone; in his place was the nice home-body in brown-and-gold jacket. It was good to know that this world was at least as gullible as mine.

*　　*　　*

I walked slowly, taking in the sights. The small houses gave way to bigger ones, and the tall buildings I'd seen from so far off came next. The crowds were thick now. I might have been back on Earth in some downtown section—maybe during the 1920s—except for a few small items. The buildings were a hodgepodge of colors: greens, reds, and purples with lots of transparent domes topping them off. The grapefruit cars looked cockeyed, although they seemed to roll okay. Trains rode at street level in transparent tunnels and were just seats, floors, and passengers, no metal bodies. Clothes ran to a lot of colors. I wondered what had happened to the gray folks and the blue boys. The only guys who might have been cops were out on the street directing traffic; they were dressed in bright yellow uniforms. I knew one thing: I didn't feel right at home here.

I moved along with the crowd, which was growing thicker by the minute.

On the Control World viewscreens had pushed the newspaper into the history books and off the streets. But like Earth this place had newspapers. I stopped at a stand, took in the headlines, the smaller print. Every third or fourth word made some kind of sense, just as on the one crumpled sheet I'd already gone over. I bent closer to give it a bit more study.

The news vendor—a short fattish guy—spoke. Whatever he said was lost on me.

I grinned at him and moved on.

The crowd carried me along with it. I stopped acting like a tourist, lost track of the sights, and let the Chairman's mind do its stuff.

Three languages. Each a dottering oldster. No longer used on their own worlds except in the study of classical lit. And here they were, all tangled together. Along with maybe a touch of Intergalactic, to boot. I didn't have time to sign up for a crash course in the local lingo. The Chairman's mind would have to do.

I started from scratch, flipped through each language one at a time. The words and phrases spun by too fast for the conscious mind to catch. I didn't sweat it, was used to the Chairman's tricks by now. I gave the orders, the Chairman's mnemonics system did the rest, catalogued words, slang, idioms, grammar, and syntax. Everything was broken down to its constituent parts, filed away for safekeeping in the unconscious. I tossed in a text on Intergalactic, the official lingo of the Galactic Arm. I'd have tossed in the kitchen sink too if I'd thought it would do any good. I had to be able to communicate, know what was going on around me. Or I was sunk.

I came up for air, looked around me.

The crush was lessening, the crowd starting to thin out. Men and women were streaming into the buildings, riding off in the transparent tube.

I wasn't ready to face this world alone yet. I wanted a crowd around, one in which I could hide.

The loudspeaker was coming from somewhere ahead of me. The words seemed to fly over the crowd like stray pigeons—unnoticed.

The sound drew me.

I shuffled along the pavement, sidestepping people who got in my way. I was starting to sweat under my brown-and-gold-striped jacket, either from the strain of using the Chairman's drill, the heat, or the general pickle I was in.

The roadway was full of the little bubbletops now and larger buses that vaguely resembled caterpillars. They made a sweet racket. Pedestrians babbled at each other. Sirens sounded from some other part of the city. Over it all I tried to follow the loudspeaker's rumble.

I turned a corner. The tall buildings became squatter here, the wide streets narrower.

A block and a half away a small crowd was gathered in a vacant lot. A makeshift stage was set up, and a lone man was on it speaking through a microphone.

I went that way.

No one seemed to mind when I elbowed my way into the crowd. I stood there breathing hard for no reason at all. This bunch looked shabbier than their counterparts on the wide streets. A lot of the multicolored jackets were faded. Some of the men needed a shave.

In the sky, over to the left, a pair of round gray craft cut a streak through the pinkish sky, lost themselves behind some tall buildings.

I sighed, turned an ear to the speaker's words. They were coming out loud and clear, amplified by the microphone to a shout. But if they meant anything at all, I wasn't getting the message.

The rest of this audience didn't share my problem; they were nodding and murmuring and even cheered once.

More than the language was bothering me. So far everything I'd seen in the city seemed normal as pie. Even this gathering was familiar enough: some politico on the stump, a fund-raiser, possibly a revival meeting. But nothing weird, nothing like the gray folks, ghost towns, or blue boys. And it would all stay a puzzle till I got the hang of the lingo. I went back to work.

Closing my eyes, I tried to put some mental distance between myself and this crowd. Three languages in all their variations and a refresher course in Intergalactic were kicking around my unconscious, where they were doing me no good. I had to get them out in the open. The Chairman knew how. And so did I.

I activated the autohypno key.

The crowd was gone. I was alone in a vast blackness.

I said a trigger word into this blackness, and it echoed around. The data stored in my unconscious were released.

A final word and the blackness turned white. I seemed to be rising slowly to the surface of a very deep lake. Bit by bit the environment fell back into place around me.

I heard a voice. It came through the loudspeaker in a blur, the words running into each other to form one long, unintelligible sentence. The sentence began to break up into parts. The parts became words.

I opened my eyes.

The speaker was saying:

"Make no mistake about it, co-citizens, the Ludies can be anywhere. Despite our best efforts, our most stringent precautions, the Ludies continue to infiltrate, to creep across our borders. They come within our midst not as friends and brothers, but as deadly enemies. Their one aim is to destroy our just order, or undermine our cherished ways, by spreading hatred and deceit. Be on your guard, co-citizens, a Ludie may be standing next to you this very moment."

The crowd murmured. Faces turned toward each other uneasily. So did mine. The woman standing next to me appeared tired, middle-aged, overweight. She didn't look like a Ludie. I sure hoped I didn't either. The man on my right had bags under his eyes, needed a shave, had a double chin. We swapped glances. He could have been a Ludie for all I knew. I tried to look innocent; it wasn't easy.

"Co-citizens," the speaker—a short guy with a lined, puffy face and a yellow-and-purple jacket—said sternly, "be on your guard. Loose talk can lead to disaster. The locations of our airfields, our defense factories, our troop bases must remain, if we are to shield our hemisphere from the Ludie menace, a closely held secret. Beware of the stranger asking too many questions. Beware the thoughtless comment that might jeopardize our defenses, that might endanger our courageous armed forces. Beware the careless tongue that can unwarily betray—"

He went on that way. I stopped listening. This knowing the lingo was a mixed blessing. I'd been happier picturing this place as a run-of-the-mill burg, not some kind of armed camp with neighbors spying on each other. It would make my job that much tougher if what the puffy-faced guy was saying turned out to be true. Possibly it wouldn't. Maybe I'd come in the middle of some set piece, a speech from a famous play this guy was reciting. Or possibly he was a fringe nut, trying to drum up some business for his sect, cult, or whatever. Yeah, lots of maybes kicking around, and not one of them seemed too likely. I had a sinking feeling that this guy was for real, that the city, behind its neat facade, was a mess. And I was stuck with it.

At least I had a way of finding out now, wasn't walking around deaf and dumb.

Mentally, I tipped my hat to the Chairman. I'd been wrong about him. This setup in his mind had an edge on practical experience. It had just saved me from landing permanently in the soup.

There were still words I didn't get, phrases that sounded fuzzy. And I hadn't tried talking yet. But I was a lot better off than I had been ten minutes ago.

I'd been listening to the guy's pitch with only half an ear when something caught my attention. I tuned in again—real quick.

The guy was saying, "The spy report, co-citizens, is not a cheerful one. Another Ludie has been seen, working his way from the east toward the city. He has already crossed a good deal of the waste area. He is said to be extremely cunning. Our Unit Nine Defense Squad was unable to apprehend him. He is armed and considered *extremely* dangerous.

"He was first sighted at a classified production zone. Immediately, the good subcitizens sounded the alarm. The Ludie fled, in *our* direction.

"Be alert, co-citizens, for a very tall man, perhaps six feet five, and dressed entirely in black. Do not approach him yourself. Signal 444 for Defense Aid. On guard, co-citizens, on guard!"

I'd broken into a light sweat. But instead of unzipping my jacket for an airing, I tried to sink deeper inside it. They'd gotten some of the details wrong, like my height, and weren't up to date on the others, but there was no doubt who shorty was talking about.

At least I'd found out what a Ludie was:

Me.

CHAPTER

9

Block went into a chop house on Third Avenue, ordered clam chowder, a couple of roast beefs on rye, a pot of coffee. He took a small corner table by the window, watched the traffic roll by as he ate. After the Control World the cars and trucks seemed as old hat as a chariot, but somehow reassuring. He might have the Chairman's mind tucked away inside him, but for all intents and purposes he was still Ross Block. At least he hoped so. What he might become later was anyone's guess. At the moment he had other problems.

One of Block's questions about Pabst-Hasting's plans had been answered. Only it wasn't the answer he especially wanted to hear. He'd turned thumbs-down—obviously—on going legit, ditched McCoy and gone underground. Great. What Block didn't know was why. Pabst had been near the top on the Control World. What would motivate him now? The Chairman hadn't put much effort into finding out what made Pabst tick. But the advice he'd dished out was on tap, and Block ruffled through it now.

By the time he was on his third cup of coffee Block knew a little more. The skinny man's advice had often resulted in his being named director, regent, or overseer of some world, Galactic military, economic, or penal system, or all-powerful committee. So maybe, like any other politician, what Pabst wanted was power, and when he got that, more power. Maybe the only difference between Van-see and Pabst was that the former tried a coup to achieve his ends, while the latter worked inside the system. Van-see, trusted adviser to the Chairman, had only succeeded for a short time in his plot to place a false Chairman in power. Block and Siscoe had seen to that. Now the real Chairman lived on only in their minds. Van-see had lost his gamble. But the system was gone now. And Pabst was on his own.

Block paid his check, went outside. After a while he managed to flag down a cab and rode over to Forty-Seventh Street.

His car was still sitting in the garage, and would do so for the next five years as long as Block's bank kept paying the bills. He hadn't driven in over a year. But he hadn't lost his touch, either.

Block steered the car out onto the street just like any other citizen and pointed its nose south, toward the Brooklyn Bridge.

The neighborhood hadn't changed much. Trees lined both sides of the block, the shrubbery and lawns were well cared for. Neither refuse nor graffiti marred the environment. The whole area was a monument to clean living, lots of money, and the Sanitation Department.

He parked in the driveway, walked through a pile of yellow and brown leaves to the three-story white frame cottage, put his finger on the bell, and rang it.

The door opened presently and he was looking at Sally Neil/Siscoe/Hastings-Pabst. A lot of history for a girl with whom he'd gone to grade school. But a couple of things had happened to Block too.

"Sally."

She squinted at him. Recognition came, and she broke into a huge smile. "Hey, it's Ross, isn't it?"

Block grinned back. "Uh-huh."

"Come on in."

He followed her into the house. She was a bit on the heavy side, but still attractive: blond hair, big bosom, wide hips; she wore a green dress with a round, frilly collar. He knew that both Siscoe and Pabst had fallen for her. She looked good, but not quite that good. Siscoe's memory was part of Block's mind too now—an advantage over the last time he'd been here. He shuffled through Siscoe's memories till he came to Sally. The pertinent details were there, all right. And he almost blushed. Block decided—gallantly—to put a lid on this part of the relationship; it was none of his business. They hit the living room.

"Take a load off," Sally said with a wave of her hand.

He chose the sofa.

"Get you something?" she asked.

"Uh-uh. Good to see you again, Sally."

"Yeah, you too."

"It's been a whole year, hasn't it?"

"Not as long as last time."

She seated herself across from him.

"Not as long," he admitted.

"So what happened?" she asked. "I kept waiting for your story, you know, about P.S. 67; the one you said I'd be in. Looked through the *Register* every day for a month. Did I miss it or what?" She grinned at Block good-naturedly.

He grinned back. "You didn't miss it. Boss killed the piece. Too insignificant. Sorry, Sal, I'm just a hired hand; I don't make policy."

"S'okay. I'll get famous some other way."

"It *was* a good idea."

"Yeah. So what about your name? I didn't see that either. You got fired or something?"

"Or something."

"Yeah?"

"Took a breather. A year off."

"No kidding?"

"Uh-huh."

"How come?"

"To write a book."

"Gee. I'm impressed."

"Nothing big. Just bread-and-butter stuff."

"Like what? A novel?"

"Uh-uh. Nonfiction."

"Yeah?"

"About business."

"Business?"

"How it works. How to make a buck. The angles."

"You know about *that*?"

"Finding out."

"So how's it going?"

"Can't complain. It's about two-thirds done. Still researching the last part."

"Yeah?"

He nodded.

"So what brings you here?"

"The book."

She laughed. "Come on."

"Really."

"You gonna ask *me* about *business*?"

"Not you."

"Who then?"

"Your husband."

"Charley?"

"Sure."

"That beats everything. What made you pick *him*?"

"Why not?"

"He's not *somebody*. I mean, we do okay, but Charley's no millionaire."

"He runs a pretty big business, Sally."

"Not anymore, he don't."

"What happened?"

"He gave it up."

"Yes?"

"Starting another line, I guess."

"Doing what?"

She shrugged. "We don't talk much about his work."

"Well, that's what I want to know about."

"I don't get you."

"What he's gone into, how he's managing. How his experience at McCoy is helping him now."

"So you *knew* about his switch?"

"Sure. That's what gave me the idea. Thought it might be fun interviewing your husband."

"That's it, huh?"

"That's it."

Sally looked embarrassed. "Gee, I don't know what to tell you."

"What is it?"

"Charley isn't here."

"No?"

"He's somewhere on the road."

"Where?"

"He didn't say."

"Not a hint?"

"Nope. It's business, see? Charley left last week, said he'd be doing a lotta travelin', getting this new line of his started."

"When's he expected back?"

"A month, maybe two. Depends on how things go."

"No way to reach him?"

"Nope."

"Not even in an emergency?"

"I'm used to it. Charley's business, you know, always had him goin' on trips. Sometimes to Europe even. I always told him, don't worry about me, I can take care of myself, right? Well, nothin's ever come up I couldn't handle."

"House never burned down, huh?"

She laughed. "Not yet."

"He ever phone?"

"Sure."

"Often?"

"Depends."

"On what?"

"His mood, I guess. Usually, he calls, maybe, once, twice a month."

"Can I leave a message with you?"

"Sure."

"Tell him I've been here, that I want to see him."

"He *knows* you?"

"Uh-huh."

"How'd *that* happen?"

"I dropped in to see him."

"Last year?"

"Yes. About the P.S. 67 piece. We had a chat."

"That's news to me."

"It was no big deal. Thought he might give me a line on some of our old classmates. Marty Nash used to work for the firm."

"Whaddya know."

"Small world, eh?"

"I'll say."

"Tell him Van-see's dead."

"Who's that?"

"A mutual friend."

"Funny name. Jap?"

"Something like that. Tell him Lix-el's running the show now."

"*Who?*"

"Lix-el."

"Jeez, what kinda name is *that*?"

"It's like the other."

"Hey, what gives? You got some kinda proposition for Charley?"

"Sort of," Block admitted.

She grinned. "No one tells me anything."

"Just business."

"Yeah, business. What happened to this book of yours?"

"That too. Ask him to call me, okay?" Block fished his wallet out of a pocket, pulled out one of his cards, wrote "Van-see" and "Lix-el" on the back, gave it to her. "So you don't forget. Tell him I want to make a deal."

"A deal."

"Uh-huh."

"Charley'll know what you mean?"

"Hope so."

"You in with those Japs?"

"One of them."

"This gets deeper and deeper!"

Block grinned. "You don't know the half of it."

"If it's business, I won't understand it anyhow."

"It's business."

Midafternoon in Brooklyn. Block left Hastings's suburban paradise, returned to the workaday world. The neat houses with their two-car garages fell behind him as he drove. In their place, worn dilapidated brownstones squatted on the streets, along with overflowing trash cans and stray bits of refuse that seemed permanently lodged in the pavements. Small, dingy groceries which extended credit and sold at top prices ruled the corners. Candy stores with bookie joints in back all but excluded kids in search of comic books and ice-cream cones: That turf belonged to the bettors.

Few trees decorated the streets. This was a people's domain. They spilled out of their houses, onto the stoops, sidewalks, roadways; kids frolicked in the gutters—wrestled, played ball or tag, shot the breeze— while oldsters took possession of the stoops, chatting or idling. And all the while box radios blared, beat out their deferred promise of excitement, love, wealth.

Block turned some more corners, hit the swank shopping center of downtown Brooklyn, rode by the plush mannequins gesturing invitingly through their show windows, giving the old come-on to passersby. Worlds within worlds. But not as many worlds as were bobbing around in his head.

What he needed now was time to sort them all out, to make sense of the Chairman's mind. He didn't want another fracas on his hands—not just yet.

It was up to Pabst, of course. But somehow Block didn't think Pabst would roll over and play dead just for the asking. At least Block had given him something to worry about. The names left with Sally would have to shake the offworlder. He'd know that Block was privy to the Chairman's mind, that his last exposure to the silver sphere had taken hold. And Pabst would know Block had managed to reach the Control World too. That might give him pause, make him think twice. Earth was small potatoes compared to the galaxies. Block had mentioned a deal. Pabst should want to check it out.

But would he?

Block didn't know, couldn't afford to sit back and find out. He had to be ready for any eventuality.

And, maybe, with the Chairman's mind riding shotgun, he would be.

Block turned the wheels of his car toward the Williamsburg Bridge and Manhattan.

CHAPTER
10

The crowd was breaking up, the speech over.

I began slowly to move with it. I wondered if cozy little get-togethers like these were going on all over this burg. And what other means of communication—besides newspapers—the natives of this world had. I wondered too if and when they'd come up with my right description. Somewhere along the line I had to ditch the jumpsuit and take a crack at speaking the local lingo. That would be the test, all right. But this wasn't quite the place for it.

I left the lot, stepped back onto the street.

A hand touched my elbow. I turned, looked down.

He was short, skinny, almost bald, with a large nose and a large pair of ears. His chin was pointy. He looked to be somewhere in his mid-sixties. He wasn't dressed in yellow shirt and green slacks this time. And he didn't have on a carbon copy of my jumpsuit either. But it wasn't too tough recognizing him. This was the little guy who'd played havoc with my mind, broadcast a preview of the blue boys at me, showed me where to duck. My unknown benefactor, in the flesh.

He was wearing a long blue-and-orange jacket, purple pants, and a small yellow peaked cap—a conservative enough get-up for these parts, from what I'd seen.

What he hadn't projected in his thought image were the purplish veins in his nose, his bloodshot eyes, the slight tremor in his hands. I knew the signs. The only things missing were the bar stool and shot glass.

"Please," he said, "we must hurry."

"Hurry where?" I said. And broke into a king-sized grin. The Chairman's mind had scored again. My first words in the local lingo and they'd come out as neat and clean as if I were a native.

"You think this a jest?" the little guy asked.

"Private joke," I told him. "You wouldn't get it. What's our rush?"

He was steering me by the arm, back toward the big, multicolored buildings, wide streets, crowds and traffic.

"They seek you."

"Yeah, so I noticed."

"You do not understand," he said breathlessly. "They will close down the entire city."

"Close down?"

"It will grind to a halt."

I looked around. The crowd was still with us, if anything growing denser again as we approached the main drag. Traffic clogged the arteries. Horns, engines, and bells joined in the din that had me thinking I was back on Broadway and Forty-second Street.

"Place seems to be jumping," I pointed out.

"You will see."

"Yeah?"

"Please. You must trust me."

That was putting it mildly. So far the little guy was the only one on this world who seemed the least bit friendly.

"Who are you?" I said.

"I am Worts."

That told me nothing.

"They're closing down this burg just to nab *me*?"

He gave me a yes.

"Because I'm a Ludie?"

"No, my friend, that is a mere cover story."

"Then why?"

"Because you are an offworlder."

"That bothers them?"

"It is a crime."

"Great."

"The Power must have things just so."

"The Power?"

"The supreme ruling body."

"Already I don't like them."

Worts smiled faintly. "You would not be the first to *think* that. But few would dare say so."

"The Power runs a tight ship, huh?"

"The Power is everywhere."

The train rushed along in its transparent tube.

I sat back in my seat, eyed the scenery. The tall buildings didn't last long. Small houses—each a different color—hurtled by outside. The train made two stops. Passengers got on and off. They didn't bother looking our way. The small houses vanished, were replaced by a stretch of green: trees, bushes, flowers, lots of lawn—a park of some kind. I could see the tops of buildings beyond it. Things seemed ordinary enough.

The little guy, Worts, sat beside me fidgeting. He seemed nervous as hell. I couldn't blame him. If the Power was really going to swoop down on me any second, Worts would be better off somewhere else. Only I was beginning to have my doubts. I wondered if a city this size *could* be turned off.

"Worts," I said.

The little man jumped. "You should not use my name here," he whispered.

"Train bugged?"

"No, not to my knowledge."

"So?"

He nodded his head at our fellow passenger. "You can never tell who might be listening."

"Yeah, but *you* can."

"I cannot."

"Come on, Worts, what are you trying to hand me?"

"It is true. My ability is circumscribed."

"You did okay with me."

"I was fresh then."

"You get stale?"

"I burn out, my friend. What I do is no easy matter. I must build up to it, conserve my energy for weeks in advance. Then I spend it all in a projection flash. It is like an explosion. I can barely contain the energy. But it dissipates swiftly, swiftly. Last night, it was all I could do to warn you of the Strike Force attack."

"The blue boys."

He nodded. "I focused on them, was able to divine their intentions. But I could not reach you. My energy was too feeble."

"You made me dream."

"Yes. Your barriers were down. You slept. It was easier for me. But I did not know if you could comprehend my message."

"I got it."

"Thank goodness."

I said, "You found me just now, Worts, found me in this gigantic city, were able to pinpoint me in a crowd. That's no mean trick, pal."

"Do you think I would have risked all by coming in person if there were any other way to reach you? I could read your location, no more. I exhausted my-self in this final effort. I am burned out, my friend."

"Why go to all this trouble, Worts?"

"You are an investment, Siscoe."

The train rocked from side to side, left the park behind. Tall white stone buildings sprang up on both sides of us. The train slowed, rolled into a station.

"You know my name, huh?"

"It was in the forefront of your consciousness when I first made contact."

"That's the best you can do—the forefront?"

Worts shrugged. "What do you expect?"

"The works. Where I was born, what I've been up to all these years, what's on my mind—stuff like that."

"What I have is a gift, one that has rescued you from certain torture and death."

"I'm not complaining."

"These other things are quite beyond me."

The train stopped, doors opened with a rush. Again, passengers entered and exited. No blue boys. No one even glanced at us. If the city was shutting down tight in an all-out effort to nail me, it was taking its own sweet time about it.

The doors hissed closed. We were on our way again. I was beginning to wonder if the little guy was strictly on the up-and-up, or if he was trying to pull something. I couldn't begin to imagine why or what. But then I couldn't imagine anything about this world either. It was a clean slate as far as I was concerned. And Worts looked like a better bet than the blue boys anyday.

I said, "This world got a name?"

"Xcroth."

I ran it through the Chairman's mind. I was starting to feel more chummy toward the Chairman by the minute. Alone I didn't have a prayer. But with

the Chairman along for the ride I just might manage
to save my skin.

There was nothing in the Chairman's mind about
Xcroth.

"It always have that name?" I asked.

Worts nodded. "As far as I know. We are in South
Xcroth."

"There's a North, too?"

"Assuredly."

"That's all, just those two?"

"The globe is split between them."

"Friendly, I hope?"

A crooked smile appeared on his face. "The Ludies
come from the North."

The buildings outside got bigger, whiter. The scenery began to look more ritzy with each station we
passed. The passengers were changing too. They
seemed better dressed than their counterparts of a
half hour ago, maybe even better fed. Some carried
briefcases, others attaché cases; Worts and I didn't
exactly look like interlopers, but we weren't one of
the homegrown products either.

I glanced over at Worts. The little guy had a large
hanky out, was mopping his brow. His hand was
shaking.

I said, "We almost where we're going?"

"Soon."

"Expect trouble?"

He shrugged.

"Where are we?"

"The Hub. It is the center of commerce. And of
government."

"Shouldn't we be heading in the opposite direction?"

"Provisions have been made for our safety. Provided we reach our friends."

His voice came out weak and uncertain. With his

talents on the blink, this Worts didn't inspire much confidence.

"I've got friends, huh?"

"You do now."

"They wouldn't be a tall fat guy and a redheaded dame?"

The color drained from Worts's face; he stared at me. "How did you know of them?"

I grinned at him. "The dream, pal. They were in the dream you sent me."

"I . . . I had not intended—"

"Leaked through, huh?"

"It is the pressure . . ."

We were rolling into a station. Worts peered out at the white platform, stiffened. I looked too, saw nothing but a crowd of passengers.

The little guy was on his feet as if his seat had turned red-hot. "Come—we must hurry."

I came. I didn't have to be asked twice.

Doors hissed open. We left with the crush.

"This way," Worts murmured.

We used the far door, stepped out onto the street.

White granite buildings loomed over us, obscuring half the sky. The street was a wide white ribbon, curving between the buildings. Pedestrians clogged the sidewalks; small bubbletops filled the roadways. As far as I could tell things were going full-blast.

I said, "What was it back there?"

"Police spies."

"Yeah?"

I must have looked skeptical. Worts turned to me, annoyance in his voice. "Time is critical now. You must suspend your disbelief, Siscoe, if we are to survive. You must put your absolute trust in me."

"Survive?"

Worts tugged at my arm, and we trotted along the pavement.

"Siscoe, you are about to witness an alarm ten alert."

"That's bad, huh?"

"Bad—for us. My risk is great. We shall be shot on sight."

"You too?"

"I am with you, am I not?"

We stopped at a contraption that looked like an old-time stand-up microphone. A row of pushbuttons ran under the mike. Worts went to work on the buttons. He spoke a few sentences into this device, turned, and we were off again.

I asked, "What was that?"

"Communo-tube."

"Getting directions?"

"Giving them. Our friends now know our whereabouts. They will attempt to aid us. We left the train two stops short of our destination. We will have to improvise."

"Improvise?"

"To save ourselves."

The sirens began to wail.

CHAPTER

11

Block pulled into the *Register*'s parking lot. His slot was taken by a Buick. He parked in an empty space, climbed out.

Old Hank, the lot attendant, shuffled through the door of his gatehouse to see who it was. His eyes widened.

"Mr. Block!" he gasped.

Block nodded pleasantly.

"Thought you was dead!"

"Just gossip."

"They been huntin' for you high and low, Mr. Block."

"I'm sure."

"Police been here, too."

"Uh-huh."

"You all right?"

"Fine, Hank."

"Where you been?"

"Traveling."

"You don't say?"

"Got to see the world sometimes, right, Hank?"

"Suppose."

Block waved a so long and started for the *Register*

building. Hank stood staring after him. If he didn't buy my tale, Block thought, what would the pros up in the office make of it? Of course, he had a better one cooked up for them and a real lulu for the boss. But would he manage to persuade anyone? And did it matter? He decided it did. He wasn't ready to cut his worldly ties yet, to become a citizen in good standing of the galaxies. He might be top dog at the Galactic Arm, but so far he didn't feel it. And maybe he never would. What he felt now was disjointed, out of focus, a spectator at his own life.

Block went through the revolving door and into the lobby, his footsteps echoing over the marble floors. The building's familiar odor enveloped him. He was home and a tourist at the same time. The Chairman's mind seemed to be looking over his shoulder.

The elevator carried him up to the sixth floor. He stepped out into the city room.

Clamor and tumult buzzed around him. Nothing had changed. It was as though he'd only gone out for a quick bite and then hustled right back. Reporters sat at their word processors, spinning out their daily yarns. Editors fiddled with copy, barked orders over phones that were never idle, seemed always to be ringing or pressed against someone's ear. Copy boys, reporters, editors clogged the aisles, weaved through thick layers of cigarette, pipe, and cigar smoke. Pale light filtered through unwashed windows. Block wondered how he'd been able to stand it for all those months.

He started walking down the main aisle. Ben Cohen's office was at the other end of the floor. Like some huge engine running out of gas, the city room began to grind to a halt. Heads turned toward him. Fingers froze over keyboards. Conversations stopped in midsentence. Only the jangling of phones remained undisturbed. He'd hoped the smoke and press of work might hide him. No such luck. He passed his desk and saw that not everything had remained the same: A stranger sat at it. Block heard his name being called. He didn't stop, just waved, and kept on his way.

A figure loomed up before him, Joe Sullivan—balding, large, stocky, with watery blue eyes—the guy who a year ago had been digging into Nick Siscoe for Block. About Siscoe, Block knew all there was to know. But Joe was too much a friend to ignore.

"Ross."

"Joe."

"Jesus, Ross—" Joe was speechless.

"Don't tell me," Block said. "You figured me for a goner?"

"Ross, so help me, we *all* did. What in God's name, *happened*?"

"Had to go away, Joe."

"Had to?"

"I stumbled across something—"

"That Siscoe thing?"

"Not that."

"What?"

"Joe, it didn't have anything to do with my assignment. I just stumbled across it."

"You had us worried, Ross."

"Sorry, couldn't help it. Orders from on high."

"The paper?"

"Higher."

"Christ, Ross."

"Listen—" By now there was a crowd gathering around them, one getting larger by the second. Block saw faces with whom he'd shared drinks, assignments, assorted woes; they were all peering at him, pressing in. As good a time as any to uncork his prime cover story—such as it was. "I'll tell you as much as I can," Block said. "It won't be much. I was kicking around on this story and not getting very far when I got wind of something—quite accidentally—that just about blew my mind. It was too hot to touch. Nothing I could break, not then, not now. I turned what I had over to the right people—they work in Washington. Maybe I should've just phoned it in, an anonymous tip. It would've saved me a lot of headaches. But I showed up in person. And that was that. They told me what to do and I did it—no questions asked. Mostly it meant staying holed up, out of harm's way, and not getting in *their* way. I did some small jobs for them a couple of times. That was about it." He paused, filled his lungs with stale air, went on. "It took a while—too long—but it's over now, gone and done with. I'm back, not much the worse for wear, and glad of it. That's it. I'm not supposed to talk about any of this. It sounds whacky anyway."

"Ross?" It was Sy Goldman. "These government guys, they were feds, CIA?"

"Something like that."

"They kept you prisoner?"

"Not exactly."

"But you couldn't just walk away?"

"Uh-uh."

"This thing was a national security matter?" Goldman asked.

"Sy—" Block said.

"A lotta crap," Pete Franklin said, "is buried under that heading, you know that, buddy?"

Ellen Speck said, "Ever hear of the U.S. Constitution, Ross? You've got certain rights."

"Why'd you knuckle under, Block?" Franklin demanded. "They got something on you, too?"

Block held up a hand. "Cut it out, guys. You know I can't—"

"Ross," Ellen said, "you *do* have some responsibilities as a reporter. One is to uphold—"

"Come on, Ellen," Block said. "I'm trying to live up to my responsibilities; don't make it tough for me."

"This agency—" Franklin began.

"Sorry. No interviews, Pete."

"Listen, Block—"

"And the press conference," Block said, grinning, "is permanently postponed."

Goldman said, "You can't just stonewall on this, Ross."

"Sure I can. Look, guys, this thing took a year out of my life. And if I put up with it, there must've been a damn good reason. The story's finished, *kaput*. I've sat on it this long, I sure as hell won't hand it over to someone else."

"How about a hint?" Ed Clark grinned.

"A hint could land me in the clink," Block said. "Have a heart, guys. I gotta go see Ben."

Block pushed his way through the crowd.

Ellen Speck called after him, "This isn't England. There is no official secrets act here!"

Franklin yelled, "It ain't Russia, either, buddy."

Block shook his head, kept going. The murmur behind him rose to a nice angry babble. His story seemed to have laid an egg. Maybe he'd've done better just keeping his mouth shut. He didn't know. But if nothing else, he'd found out what it's like being on the wrong end of a reporter's questions: not so hot.

Block pushed open the door to Cohen's office without knocking.

Cohen looked up from his desk. He was a short heavyset man with a round face, balding dome, thick hairy arms, and something of a potbelly. He was sixty-two and had been city editor for twelve years.

"Ben."

Cohen's mouth slowly opened, and his cigar fell from his lips to the desk.

"I don't believe it," he said.

"Hardly believe it myself," Block said.

"You real, son, or have I had one too many for lunch?"

"I could pinch myself and find out."

"Don't bother. I like it better if you're a spook. Come in. And shut the door."

Cohen retrieved his cigar, stuck it back in his mouth. Block sat down in a straight chair.

"Good to see you, Ben."

"You too. You're looking okay, Ross."

"Thanks."

"For a spook."

"Oughta see me levitate."

"Walk through walls, I bet?"

"Sure. We all do."

"Must be a great life."

"Not exactly *life*, Ben."

"Yeah." Cohen relit his cigar, puffed some smoke. "This better be good, son. Besides all the time, energy, and dough this paper spent on finding you, besides all the cops we dragooned into hunting for your body, there was also the little matter of the grief we lavished on your behalf."

"I can imagine."

"Yeah. Lots of grief."

"I'm sorry, Ben."

"Figured you were pushing up the daisies somewhere. That the Nash business had done you in."

"Logical enough assumptions."

"That girl of yours, Nora, she called me. Back when you first vanished. Very upset. Couldn't blame her."

Block nodded.

"But here you are, alive and kicking."

"Those are the breaks."

"Yeah. *So what the hell happened?*"

Block said, "That's what the guys outside wanted to know."

"They would. You've got more friends out there than you know."

"Had."

"Yeah?"

"Lots of them aren't too pleased with what I told them."

"Which was?"

"While looking into the Nash thing—which I neglected to identify, incidentally—I ran across something else, some hanky-panky, espionage, treason, you name it. I took it to the feds, who shook my hand and put me under wraps for a year while they cleaned up the mess. That's what I told them."

"Is it true?"

"No."

Cohen shook his head. "At least you're honest—with me."

"Can't lie to the boss, can I?"

"Well, what was it, Ross?"

"The Nash business."

Cohen nodded. "Didn't I tell you? Said you were playing with dynamite. What happened?"

Block sighed. "Wish I could tell you."

"Wish?"

"Uh-huh."

"What *is* this, Ross?"

"I don't remember any of it."

Cohen glared at him.

"I blacked out."

"Come on, Ross."

"I spent a lot of time on the Bowery, Ben, panhandling, trying to raise enough change for the next drink. On good days I almost remembered my name."

"Bullshit."

"I wish it were. There's a guy sweeps up at the Men's Shelter, his name's Knobby—a nice old duffer—he'll vouch for me. I used to hang out there. Neat, eh?"

Cohen was staring at Block, his face flushed. "You expect me to swallow that?"

Block shrugged. "I can give you chapter and verse. The Bowery was my home for the better part of a year, Ben. Just walk up and down the street, ask the barkeeps, the liquor-store clerks, they'll remember me."

"We had the cops out looking for you."

"Sure, the cops were looking for a clean-cut reporter type, maybe floating face down in the Hudson, not some derelict in a Bowery flophouse."

Cohen scowled at him. "What did you do, fall down and hurt your head? An accident?"

"No accident."

"*Well?*"

"This Nash thing."

"Yeah?"

"It caught up with me."

"That so?"

"I know it sounds a bit nutty, Ben."

"Only a bit? You're an optimist."

"I'm sorry."

"Dumb is what it sounds like. You're insulting my intelligence."

"Just listen, will you, Ben?"

"So who isn't listening?"

"I made progress on the Nash killing."

"The body *was* Nash, I take it?"

"Yes, Nash. I tied him to an outfit called McCoy, an export-import firm. A lot of their business seems to've been aboveboard, and most of the employees—as far as I could tell—were honest enough. But McCoy had another operation going, off the books, and that was as crooked as they come."

"What was it?"

Block shrugged. "You name it. Dope. Illegal arms. Maybe just tax fraud. I didn't get that far. But it was big."

"Big."

"That's the way it looks. A father-daughter team—the Pavels—who worked for McCoy tumbled to the racket. They had a chat with me and haven't been heard from since."

"Dead?"

"Uh-huh."

"But not you."

"They slipped me something. In a drink or food. Maybe it was supposed to knock me off. I don't know. Killing a reporter isn't so hot, gets everyone in dutch. Maybe they just meant to do something to my mind, screw it up, turn me into a vegetable. The right drug would do it. Who'd be the wiser? That, in any case, is when I blacked out."

"Do these 'they' have a name?"

"Sure. Charles Hastings, for one; he ran the outfit."

"Ran? What happened, he retire?"

"Only in a manner of speaking.

"Don't play games, Ross, not now."

"Sorry. Being back here has me kind of high. It's like this. I came up for air a little over a week ago. The haze lifted, I knew who I was and what Hastings had done to me. Maybe I wasn't thinking too clearly yet, but I braced Hastings. He and a hired hand—a Lew Jenks—followed me to the Men's Shelter, of all places. The pair had guns. There was a tussle and I got the better of them."

Cohen looked incredulous. "Coming off a one-year drunk?"

"That's what they figured, too. I was lucky, I guess, caught 'em from behind."

Cohen puffed at his cigar. "They *let* you get behind them?"

"They thought I'd fainted, Ben. Almost did, too."

"That's one for the books, kid."

"I laid 'em out, Ben. You can check with a Detective Loufer, 197th Precinct."

"You called the cops?"

"Uh-huh."

"What happened?"

Block shrugged. "I blew it, that's what. It was my word against theirs. They were somebody and I was the next best thing to a skid-row bum. The cops let them go. I was lucky they didn't chuck me in the slammer."

Cohen sighed. "You sure screwed that up, son!"

"You're telling me? I was still woozy, no doubt about it. I should've waited, not gone running off to confront Hastings. My mistake. I tipped my hand."

Cohen grinned. "Thought you were gonna sober up, huh? Must have scared the pants off 'em."

"Why not? I knew about Nash, the Pavels. If I got back on my feet, became respectable again, got the paper behind me, and kept digging, no telling what I might come up with."

Cohen shook his head. "I don't know, Ross—"

"Just listen, Ben. You asked if Hastings had retired."

"Yeah."

"He's gone, Ben."

"Gone?"

"Uh-huh."

"You mean *skipped*?"

"Yep. And he's junked the firm."

"He *what*?"

"No more McCoy, Ben. They closed shop."

"Just like that?"

"*Literally* overnight."

"How *could* they, Ross?"

"Wasn't easy, I'll bet. Lost a mint, too. You'll admit it looks a bit suspicous?"

"Yeah, I'll admit that."

"Thanks."

"*Provided* what you say is on the level."

"Check it out, Ben."

"Don't worry, I'm going to."

"Remember, they only dumped the legit end of the business. The rest still goes marching on. The story's there. It's ours for the taking. And it's *big*."

Cohen nodded cautiously.

"Ben."

"Yeah?"

"I want this story."

"I kind of figured that."

"I want all the dope our guys dug up on Nash last year. I want McCoy put through a sieve—the works. And our overseas guys to nose into McCoy's foreign ties. And I want to head it all up."

"You don't want much, do you?"

"Not much, Ben. Just what I've earned."

CHAPTER
12

Worts stood stock still, his face turning a disagreeable ash-gray. He looked no worse than any cadaver on the way to an autopsy.

"Too soon," he whispered.

The blare of the sirens was all around us now, careening off the tall buildings, bleating out of doorways, echoing down the twisting streets.

"This way," Worts said, breaking into a run.

We headed for the next corner.

Around us the city was going haywire. Bubbletops screeched to a halt in midlane; drivers leaped out, raced away. Pedestrians aborted their strolls, took to their heels like track stars. Worts and I were going great guns, but next to some of these speedsters we were just crawling. Buildings, I saw, were emptying out too, and others filling up.

We rounded a corner. The pavement branched off into two narrow streets. Worts chose the one to the right.

"What the hell's happening?" I growled.

"The alert—"

His words were lost. Loudspeakers had opened up over the sirens, were blasting away.

"Report to nearest Processing Shelter. Report to nearest Processing Shelter . . ."

A metallic voice began slowly counting backward. "Fifty, forty-nine, forty-eight . . ."

What was left of the crowd around us picked up speed as if given a collective jolt of white-hot electricity. A poor time to be a straggler, it seemed.

Worts panted, "We must not be caught!"

I'd gotten that idea myself.

We rounded a second corner.

Over the sirens, over the dead voice counting away the seconds, a new sound made itself heard.

I looked up.

Jet balls were in the sky, sailing over the tops of buildings, hundreds of them. They began to sink down like dead weights.

Up ahead a truck pulled to a halt. Men in green uniforms piled out, unslung their weapons. One helluva fast operation.

By now Worts and I were becoming standouts. Only a few runners shared the street with us. They didn't look as if they were going to be around long.

We turned a third corner.

"Twenty-four, twenty-three, twenty-two . . ."

We were in a cobblestone alley, the only moving objects in sight. Back doors lined either side of the alley; metal grating covered them. There were no windows, no other openings. Refuse cans stood by some of these doors. They were too small to hide in.

Worts stumbled, stopped, leaned up against a doorway. His forehead was bathed in sweat.

The loudspeaker voice said, "twelve, ten, nine . . ."

"I cannot go on," Worts said. "We are too far away; it is useless."

"What's happening out there?"

His words came out weak, broken by short gasps for air. "All must . . . go to the shelters; all . . . *shall* go. None will be ... left ... on the streets. There are ... no exceptions."

"They search the buildings?"

He nodded. "Except for those designated as shelters."

"The whole city?"

Worts nodded again.

"That would take an army, pal."

"It does." Worts looked sick.

"How far are we from your friends?"

"A half link."

"We safe once we get there?"

"Yes. But it is *impossible*. We must pray that they spare us, leave the alley with our hands raised, throw ourselves on their mercy—"

"Three, two *one*."

The nice loudspeaker voice stopped. The sirens halted. No jet balls whirled overhead; they'd all landed, it seemed. I heard no sounds at all. As if someone had taken the city beyond our alley and carted it far away.

Worts and I looked at each other.

"They're not hunting you, pal," I said. "Just me. Walk away now and no one'll be the wiser."

"It is too late. You do not understand."

"Enlighten me."

"They have finished the count. Those who are not in the Processing Shelters are detained, interrogated."

"Big deal. They've got nothing on you."

"You are wrong, my friend. They have *everything*."

"I don't get it."

His eyes were wide with fear. "The brain probe, the truth serum. They cannot be withstood. The Power will know all. I shall be executed."

"Haven't you people got any rights?" I asked.

A sickly smile spread across Worts's face. "At one

time, yes. But all that is a dim memory. A state of emergency has existed for eight years now."

"Emergency?"

"Between North and South Xcroth. Both halfs of the globe are in constant readiness. We live under martial laws."

"And you figure they're planning to shoot me on sight."

"Yes."

"And you too?"

He nodded.

"And you want to give yourself up?"

"What else is there?"

"You must be crazy."

From out on the street, the stillness—which was bad enough—was replaced by something even worse: the sound of marching feet, lots of them.

"What the hell's *that?*"

"Search squads."

"Headed here?"

"They work by the drill. The houses come first."

"Then we've got some time."

"Minutes only. They will be pouring in from all sides, thousands of hunters."

I began to see why the scarecrows I'd met might think twice about visiting their good city—especially if they weren't welcome. I was thinking twice myself.

I said, "This alley goes where?"

"Not far enough."

Along with the marching feet, I heard voices now. Near the head of the alley. The last thing I needed.

I grabbed Worts by a shoulder, pushed him forward, deeper into the alley. He stumbled ahead of me, his eyes glassy, mouth half open, small gasping noises escaping between his lips.

"These friends of yours, can they still help us if we reach them?"

He nodded. "They have the means."

"That's dandy," I said. "Can they reach *us*?"

"If they knew where we were."

"Tell 'em."

"How?"

"With your mind."

"I cannot." He seemed close to tears. "I have nothing left."

"Shit." I hadn't busted out of the penal colony and risked my neck on the Control World just to end up a stiff on some two-bit backwoods planet. I had only two things going for me here: Worts and the Chairman's mind. They would have to do.

The Chairman had been worried about Ganz, had boned up on telepathy before dispatching the mind reader to the hoosegow. Everything the Chairman knew I had at my disposal.

I used the hypnotic code, activated the unconscious scanner, set up a pipeline between my conscious and unconscious mind, and began flipping through the Chairman's mind.

Outside the alley the city had come to life again. Only it was a life I could have done without. No casual footsteps, no chatting voices, no stray traffic. I heard the troops trotting off in various directions, shouted orders, doors banging open. The mission had been let out a notch, was going into double-time. And the net around us was growing tighter.

"Worts," I said.

The little guy turned.

I had my nerve gun out.

I shot him.

I propped the little guy against the wall, put my palm on his chest to hold him in place. Worts was sagging.

His eyes were open, but held as much savvy as a

clothing-store dummy's. He was drooling out of the left side of his mouth. I'd given him the lowest possible charge.

The conscious mind was shorted now, passive; the unconscious held sway. I put my trust in the unconscious.

"Worts," I said, "can you hear me?"

Something that could have been yes came through his lips.

"Contact your friends," I said. "Tell 'em where we are."

The unfocused eyes were fixed over my shoulder, probably peering into the next decade, or the last.

"Go on," I said. "Contact them. Call your friends." I shook him gently by the shoulder with my free hand. "Now," I said.

His legs buckled.

"Shit," I said.

I started my spiel over in a low persuasive voice; I sounded like a broken record. But this bit of business was all I had going for me now, the only kernel of wisdom I'd come up with in the Chairman's mind.

I wondered what kind of rescue mission Worts's pals could mount against this kind of opposition. I didn't let myself think of that. I had enough problems just getting the little guy to do his stuff.

After a while I started slapping his face, bringing him around. I'd done all I could, used up the last option. If we were going to be gunned down by the troops, Worts ought to be awake to see it. He might even want the chance to shoot back.

We moved up the alley.

The soldiers were somewhere behind us, lost around one of many curves. I could hear their voices. Nothing came from up ahead—yet.

Sounds out on the street were still going strong.

The guys who caught us would probably wind up heroes.

I had my arm around Worts's shoulder, trying to steady him. He wasn't doing so hot. He was awake, all right, but that was about all. He couldn't talk, could hardly keep on his feet. He was shaking hand and foot as though he'd just taken a dip in the Arctic. He looked older too, as if my little stunt with the stunner had put him permanently on the skids. Permanently, I figured, wasn't apt to last too long.

It came as a black speck in the sky, grew bigger as I watched, a jet-propelled ball done up in solid black.

Its drone got louder as it sank toward us.

Worts looked up, his eyes as glassy as ever. He cackled, an insane laugh that gave me goose bumps. I'd burned him out, pushed him over the edge. And all for what?

I dug my nerve gun out of its pocket. It wasn't worth beans against the firepower of a jet ball, but it was better than waiting with empty hands.

I didn't quite believe—no matter how nutty these Xcroths were—that they'd pass up the chance to give me the old third degree, put me through the wringer, and find out what my business was on their world. I couldn't see them just mowing me down. Still, Worts had seemed sure enough, and Worts ought to know. He was a native—and on good days he could even read minds. Some Worts. He cackled again as the ball settled down in the middle of the alley. It sat there like a large black egg waiting to hatch.

The green-clad troops turned a corner then, on the double. The black ball brought them up short. It was between them and us. The troops had a small arsenal of weapons with them, as though they were hunting a whole band of fugitives instead of just one. They didn't use them. What they did was look confused.

A side hatch opened in the ball.

A large, overweight, bald-headed guy climbed out. He wore a black uniform, wide black belt, high leather boots—right out of central casting. He even had a small beard.

A couple of other black-uniformed guys popped up behind him. They aimed long-necked weapons my way.

Beyond the ball more green-clad troops had joined those already there. It began to look like a convention. No one was bothering to shoot me—yet.

The fat man turned his face toward me. His lips were full, nose wide, eyebrows black and bushy. With the exception of one deep furrow in his forehead, his face was completely unlined. He addressed me in a smooth baritone: "You there!"

"Yeah?" I called back.

"Lower your weapon, put up your hands. Resistance is useless."

I looked at the fat man, at the mass of soldiers clogging one side of the alley. Carefully I lowered the nerve gun, replaced it in its pouch. I could have dropped it on the ground, but why lose a good weapon?

"Step forward. I arrest you in the name of the state."

I stepped forward.

Worts giggled and almost fell to his knees. I caught him, dragged him toward the black ball.

I had planned to go out in a blaze of glory. But here I was, as docile as a lamb. Any second I expected the troops to start jeering.

I didn't mind.

The fat man was the same guy I'd seen in Worts's dream. In full view of a couple hundred troops with orders to kill, I was being spirited off by one of Worts's cabal. And no one was raising a finger to stop me.

A funny notion began to wiggle through my skull. What if this guy wasn't a friend after all, but someone Worts had feared, tried to warn me against? What if the guy really *did* work for the state?

Our jet ball rose straight up over the city.

I stared down through the cockpit viewer at the troops—necks craned in our direction—growing smaller, the hundreds of green copters filling the streets becoming ovals, the buildings transforming themselves into small rectangles and squares.

"What did you do?" I asked the tall, bald-headed man by my side. "Hypnotize them?"

"It was not necessary." He smiled. "The Secret Police inspire respect, even from the military."

"Secret Police?" I said.

"Our color is black."

"Our?" I said.

"Allow me to introduce myself. I am Casparian."

"Casparian," I said.

"Deputy Director of the Secret Police."

I looked over at Worts. He was stretched out on the floor snoozing peacefully. The two other guys weren't paying any attention to me. One was busy piloting the ball; his partner was busy doing nothing. If this was a pinch, these guys didn't have their hearts in it.

I said, "You one of Worts's pals?"

The fat man beamed at me. "We are like brothers."

"He reached you, huh?"

Casparian nodded delightedly. "His message came through like thunder."

"That's nice," I said. "Somehow I didn't figure Worts or his pals for Secret Police."

"Actually," Casparian said, "they're not."

"But you are?"

"Oh, yes, for perhaps another hour or so."

"And then?"

"Why, then I become an outlaw just like you."

I looked at the guy, wondering if he was kidding me. He seemed serious enough.

"Think it's better on the other side?"

"Much worse," Casparian said. "I should know."

"Then why the switch?"

"For you, Siscoe. I have given up everything for you."

I peered through the viewer.

Down below was a walled structure that looked like a medieval castle. Or prison. We began to sink toward the courtyard.

"What's that?" I asked.

"Secret Police Headquarters," Casparian said.

"They sure won't think of looking for me there," I said. "Or will they?"

"Almost at once, I'm afraid. As soon as the higher echelons of the military are informed of your capture—"

"Capture?"

"Merely a figure of speech."

"Yeah, I'm sure."

"When the military hears that you have been spirited off by their archrival, the Secret Police, they shall immediately resort to the tell-eye, demand your transfer. They will, of course, be backed by the Executive Board. It is then that the discovery will be made."

"Discovery?"

"That the Secret Police had, in fact, no hand in your apprehension."

"That should shake 'em up a bit."

"You have no idea, Siscoe, how much."

* * *

We plunked down in the yard.

Worts was lifted by the two extras and carted off the ball. Casparian and I followed.

"We must make haste," Casparian said.

That was dandy with me.

We trotted across the courtyard. A couple of black-uniformed guys glanced our way. They didn't seem too interested.

Worts was literally being carried along, his feet dragging on the ground. The sight, in this place at least, caused no raised eyebrows. Some place.

We went through a side door into the building.

The trappings of yesteryear were gone. Plasto-deck walls and corridors greeted us, the first I'd seen on this world. Spotter eyes peered down at us from the ceilings. It made me feel right at home—just as if I were back on the penal world, a home I hated.

"You boys here are right up to date, aren't you?"

"Oh, yes." Casparian grinned. "The very best. Plasto-deck, spotter and tell-eyes, magneto-ears. You name it, we have it."

"But not out in the street, not in the towns or cities."

"Quite right. And most perceptive of you. All these things are the sole preserve of the Power."

"And the rest of the country?"

"Not country. Hemisphere." He shrugged. "They make do as best they can."

We rounded some more corners—all under the watchful gaze of the spotter-eyes—took the lift two flights up, entered an office.

"Home." Casparian beamed at me. "Rava!" he called.

An inner door opened and there she was: the red-headed girl, the one I'd seen with the scarecrows out in the wilds. She had on the black uniform of the

Secret Police. It looked good on her. Most anything would.

"Nothing stirring—yet," she told Casparian.

Through the doorway I saw a viewscreen, communo-relay, a battery of spotter-eye and magneto-ear receivers.

Casparian grinned at me. "Our little game so far goes undetected."

"Monitor room, huh?" I said.

"Only the best here."

Rava said, "Strip out of those uniforms." She turned to me. "You too."

Dutifully, I peeled off my jacket, unzipped my jumpsuit. I was going to miss my old suit, but not half as much as I'd miss my freedom. One of the extras began to undress Worts.

The girl went into the next room, returned with a cardboard box. Green uniforms were in it.

"We join the military." Casparian beamed and winked at me.

The girl changed in the other room. Very modest. This world was really getting me down.

"With some luck," Casparian said, "we shall actually survive this ordeal."

Casparian went into the next room. The girl came back, an okay trade.

"Small world," I said.

"Very." She was all decked out in her new greens, which looked as spiffy on her as the black getup. Mine was too tight.

I said, "Enjoy keeping tabs on me?"

"It had its moments."

"Could've saved us both some grief."

"How's that?"

"By being friendly."

"In the wastelands?"

"That's what you call it?"

She nodded. "The gray towns, the wastelands, the lost places."

"Sounds swell. Yeah, in the wastelands."

"I couldn't."

"Too shy?"

"Not sure."

"Sure?"

"What to do with you."

"Do with me?"

"Whether to kill you or not."

"What the hell's wrong with you people?" I said in disgust.

"No need to fret. You passed the test."

"Test?"

She nodded. "Did everything wrong. Why, if it weren't for Worts you would have been dead long ago."

"Good old Worts," I said.

Casparian stepped back into the room. "It is done." He beamed.

"Glad to hear it," I said. "What's done?"

"Your entrance into the building. I have erased it from the spotter-eye tapes. There will be no record of your coming here. Your disappearance will remain a mystery to the world at large. And to the Power."

"You guys tape everything?"

"As much as is necessary. Which is usually a very great deal."

"How do I get off this world?"

"That, Siscoe, is what I was hoping you would tell us."

Something that looked like a freight elevator carried the six of us down to the basement. Worts was still in slumberland. His two keepers lugged him toward the dozen parked bubbletops.

"The little guy okay?" I asked.

"Who can tell?" Casparian said.

"Sorry," I said.

Rava shrugged. "At least he gave his all in a good cause."

"Which one?" I asked.

"You."

The car we climbed into was a wide green bubble-top, the only green item in the bunch. The rest were all a uniform, dismal black.

The taller of the two stooges took the wheel.

We drove up a ramp. A wide door swung into the ceiling.

We rode out onto the deserted streets and away from the Secret Police building.

I said, "Couldn't find a better place to hide me?"

"Than what?" the fat man said.

"The goon squad back there, the Secret Police Headquarters. Brother!"

"Don't complain," Rava said. "We got out again, didn't we?"

"I think it's aged me," I said.

"Not as much as you aged poor Worts," Casparian pointed out. "Believe me, Siscoe, the situation left us no alternative. You and Worts fell short of your destination, it is as simple as that."

"Simple enough," I admitted.

"Look," Rava said.

Everyone except Worts looked.

A roadblock was up ahead, one manned by a number of green-clad armed soldiers. Our car slowed to a crawl. Casparian stuck his head out the window and exchanged a few words with the sentries. We were waved through. I let out my breath.

Casparian chuckled. "Privilege of rank. He thinks me a general. A reasonable assumption, since I wear a general's insignia. Anyone else, Siscoe, caught wearing this uniform unlawfully would be summarily executed."

"But not you, huh?"

He laughed. "Dear me, no. As Deputy Director of the Secret Police, I am not subject to the usual restraints. I could easily survive this impersonation. Or any other, for that matter. All part of the job, you understand. It is expected of me."

"That's nice," I said.

Casparian sighed. "What I couldn't survive, unfortunately, is helping you escape. The ball, you see, that is what has ruined the game."

"The ball," I said.

"Of course. Actually, Worts is at fault."

"Worts," I said.

"Absolutely. He panicked."

"He wasn't the only one, pal."

"But he should have known better. This is, after all, his world. It was imperative, Siscoe, that he remain on that train, reach the proper station. The military had only a vague description of you. It was assumed you were traveling alone. Why, in Worts's company you would have been next to invisible. And we were prepared to offer you protection, Siscoe, to escort you to safety once you made contact with our agents."

I shrugged. "Tell Worts, not me."

"Quite right. Worts has great talents. But he has never been trained in the clandestine arts. Such training might, in fact, be quite beyond him."

"Can't all be spies," I said.

"There you have it. Absolutely. But fleeing from the train and then allowing yourselves to be trapped in that alley, that, Siscoe, was sheer disaster. My agents could not reach you on foot. The military is all-supreme on such occasions, and quite efficient. During an alert only military planes and cars are allowed to roam. I can assure you, they have it down to perfection."

"Yeah, I noticed."

"So you did. Nothing takes the place of firsthand experience, does it, Siscoe?"

We slowed for another checkpoint. No one gave us the business. A general's car with six uniformed passengers didn't rate much attention. General's cars were probably a dime a dozen. What these boys were after was a lone, desperate stranger afoot and lost somewhere in the city.

I was glad that stranger wasn't me. Although I wasn't too crazy about the folks I was with, either.

Our car picked up speed. The streets were empty, except for the soldiers. There were plenty of them around. They looked just like us. The buildings, still white, were even taller.

"Yes," Casparian said, "I had no choice. If you and Worts were to be pulled from the net, I myself had to make use of the jet ball. A subordinate would not suffice. Only an official of my rank could procure a ball while an alert was in progress. I did so. They will know of it presently, if they do not already know. I can never return. But you, Siscoe, will make that up to me, won't you?"

I waved a hand. "Be my guest."

"Why, I intend to," Casparian said. "We all do."

CHAPTER
13

It took a while, but Block got what he wanted. When he left the *Register* building he carried two bulging briefcases with him. They contained whatever his colleagues had managed to dig up a year ago on Nick Siscoe, the late Marty Nash, and his employer, McCoy Export-Imports.

Old Hank stopped Block as he walked past the gatehouse and into the parking lot.

"Darn," he said. "Thought I'd dreamed you up, Mr. Block."

"Still in the flesh, Hank."

"You really travelin' like you said?"

"Uh-uh."

He lowered his voice. "Where you been?"

"Special assignment."

"Don't believe a word of it."

"Neither does anyone else."

Block went to his car, tossed the briefcases onto the back seat, and rode away from there.

So far it was easy. He was touching all the bases, making all the right moves. Only so far wasn't very far. And until he had his chat with Pabst, it wasn't worth beans.

Block sighed. And turned the car toward Queens.

He sat in his car, opposite the twelve-story red brick apartment house. He had visited it once a year ago to collect Professor Pavel and his daughter Anna. Both had worked for McCoy, had grown suspicious, figured the firm for crooked. He rode out with them to a house in the country to hunt for evidence. Pabst showed up with a couple of helpers. Exit the Pavels. And almost exit Block.

He climbed out of the car, crossed the street, went into the building.

The Pavels had lived in 7B. The name Fletcher was on the bell now. He buzzed it, waited.

"Yes?" a female voice answered through the intercom.

"My name's Ross Block. I'm a reporter for the *Daily Register*. I'm doing a story on a former tenant of this building. May I see you?"

"Sure," a voice told him.

He was buzzed into the lobby, carried up in the elevator to the seventh floor. Seven was supposed to be lucky.

She was a small, thirtyish woman in a green housedress. She invited Block in.

The place was entirely different from the last time he'd been here. The ornate antique furniture which had cluttered the Pavel's apartment was gone. Chic modern items—out of Bloomingdale's—now filled what he could see of the flat.

He gave her the same cover story he'd used on everyone else.

"The Pavels were informants," he told her, "in a crooked business scheme. They were working with the *Register* at the time of their disappearance. That was about a year ago."

"And they were living *here*?" she asked.

"7B."

"Gosh, that's spooky. They just *vanished*?"

"Uh-huh."

"You think it's *safe* here?" She sounded anxious.

"Change the lock?"

"Of course."

"It's safe."

She smiled at him. "So what can I do for you?"

"I'm interested in the Pavels' belongings."

"Their *things*."

"Uh-huh."

She wrinkled her nose. "Oh dear."

"No dice?"

"No things."

He sighed. "Figures."

"When I moved in here, Mr. Block, the place was clean as a whistle. I mean, there wasn't even a speck of dust."

"That's pretty clean."

"I'm sorry."

"The breaks. Who's the super here?"

"Mike."

"Just Mike?"

"Mike the super."

"Where's he hang out?"

"Ground floor rear. It says 'Super' on the door. You can't miss it."

Block thanked her and went down to find the super.

Mike answered on the first ring.

"Yeah?" He was a narrow-chested, hatchet-faced man in his fifties. His black hair was slicked back. He had on a denim work shirt and jeans.

Block showed him his press card.

The super looked from the card to Block. "What's this about?"

"The Pavels."

"*Them*, huh? They skipped. Owed a month's rent, too. You looking for 'em?"

"Uh-uh. His things."

"*Things?* You mean like clothes and stuff, furniture?"

"Yes."

"Got rid of 'em, mister. No place to store 'em. Look, know how much storage space costs? The guy owed rent, too. We threw out what we couldn't sell. It's gone, vamoosed."

"Gone where? Who bought it?"

He waved an arm. "Search me. That was a year ago, mister."

"You'd think," Block said, "the security deposit would've covered a month's rent."

"What's it to you?"

"Friend of the Pavels'."

"Yeah?"

"They were doing a job for me when they died."

"Died?"

"Uh-huh."

"Didn't know that."

"Not general knowledge."

"What happened?"

"Accident."

"Too bad."

Block said, "Find any papers?"

"Papers?"

"Guy was a professor. Had to have papers."

He shrugged. "What can I tell you, mister?"

"The papers could mean dough."

"Yeah?"

"*Register* was doing a story. About how some firms cut corners. Professor Pavel was researching it for us."

"That so?"

"*Register*'s still interested."

"Don't say?"

"Not a *big* story. Less than medium."

"Yeah?"

"But a story that's worth something. About three hundred bucks."

The super looked at Block, wet his lips. "I don' know . . ."

"Let's make it an even five."

"Five hundred?"

"Yep. Got it right here. No waiting. In cash."

Block fished out his wallet, removed five hundred dollar bills, stuffed them in the super's shirt pocket "Off the books. Just between you and me. An easy five, Mike. No questions asked. You won't get a bet ter deal."

"The prof, see, he *did* leave something—for safe keeping. Only he said I shouldn't give it to no one."

"He's dead, Mike."

"Yeah. And you was on the same team."

"Right."

The super carefully transferred the money from his shirt to his pants pocket.

"Prof left this with me, maybe six months before he kicked off."

"You got it here?"

"Yeah. In the basement. Don't know if it's papers though."

"What is it?"

"A trunk. A small trunk."

Dusk edged over Manhattan. Block drove through the darkening streets. Lights shone at him. Cars, buses trucks hedged him in. The streets were thick with pedestrians. He'd hit the tail end of rush hour. The crush seemed to press down on him as traffic slowed to a tired crawl. The weather was cool, but Block was breaking into a sweat. The views through his car window seemed as strange and alien as anything he'd encountered on the Control World, or remembered through the Chairman's mind. A small voice in his head kept asking him who he was and what he was doing here. He licked dry lips, wondering if he was going to hold up long enough to finish this job. He wasn't so sure anymore.

He gazed out the window. He was on Eighth Avenue in the mid-forties. Neon lights winked and beckoned, pushing their wares: girlie shows, massage parlors, adult bookstores, gay porno flicks. Street-corner hookers were out in full force, hunting up the johns. Dopesters, he knew, were loose in this crowd, peddling merchandise, their voices low, intense. Prowl cars ignored them, wheeled by in search of gaudier crimes. Block sighed, shuddered. He'd seen all these sights countless times before. Why was he letting them get to him now?

Siscoe would've done better at this, Block thought, rolled with the punches. He was somehow more pliable, adjusted quicker. But Siscoe was back on the Control World now, probably mopping up the last of the holdouts, giving Lix-el a boost up toward the Chairman's seat. The mess here was Block's baby. But he didn't have to face it alone. He had the Chairman's mind for company. Maybe *that* was the problem.

Suddenly Block reached a decision. There was nothing to being alone tonight. The Chairman's mind would only chatter at him, give him the cold sweats. He needed something to anchor him to this world, something to help keep him sane.

He turned the wheels of his car up a side street, then downtown, heading toward SoHo.

CHAPTER
14

"Good of you to come, Siscoe." His voice sounded like the rustle of dried leaves. He looked to be pushing eighty. His eyes were a clear, very cold blue. There were pouches under them, and bushy white brows on top. His nose was long, crooked, his lips two thin lines. The top of his dome was a bald oval; white hair sprouted from the back of his head, fell to his stooped shoulders. He sat in a large armchair, a slight, frail-looking figure—in a formless, gray, jumpsuit—hands folded in his lap, and he grinned at me, with what looked to be his own teeth, no mean trick.

I grinned back. "Best invitation I've gotten on this world."

"I am pleased to hear you say that. There are some who would deem Xcroth inhospitable. And doubtless there is a kernel of truth in that."

I waved away the possibility. "Just some rowdies—like the military, police, and most of your citizens."

"Yes, yes, a spirited lot. But I, in my small way, still seek to uphold the amenities."

"Very considerate."

The old geezer bowed his head. "Someone must carry on the ancient traditions."

"And that someone is you," I said.

"It is."

"And you are?"

"Targ."

"Targ," Casparian said, "was one of our leading manufacturers."

"Armaments," Targ said.

"But he is retired now," Casparian said.

"I lead a quiet life," Targ said. "My sole remaining responsibility—if it may be called that—is as president of the Manufacterers' Guild, an all but honorary title. You are in our offices now."

The offices were in the penthouse of one of the taller white buildings in the area. The roof was a glass dome, the walls glass panels. A hundred and ten floors below, I could see the city streets winding off into the distance.

I turned back to the old man. He, Casparian, Rava, and I were the only occupants of the top story. Worts and his pair of keepers had dropped us off at a side entrance and ridden away for parts unknown.

Targ leaned forward, licked his lips, peered at me with his cold eyes. "How much, Siscoe, do you know of our world?"

"Not a damn thing."

"Then what brings you here?"

"A slipup."

"I beg your pardon?"

"A crossed wire, possibly, a short circuit, maybe sabotage. Who knows? Whatever it was, here I am."

"In other words," Casparian said, "your visit to Xcroth is entirely unplanned."

"Yeah, that's what it is, all right, unplanned."

"I find that," Targ said, "hard to believe."

I shrugged. "Suit yourself."

"He's telling the truth," Rava said. "I was there shortly after he arrived. He was a babe in the woods;

you could see he was thoroughly unbriefed. Why, he even tried to make contact with the wastelanders."

Casparian nodded. "Worts rescued him repeatedly. As far as Worts could tell, he knows nothing of our world."

"I see," Targ said. "Then perhaps you can tell me, Siscoe, where you were heading when the good Worts intervened."

"Here."

"The Hub?"

"Yeah, the Hub."

A thin smile crossed Targ's lips; his raspy voice turned syrupy. "And why was that, Siscoe?"

"Tall building," I said.

"I beg your pardon."

"You can see 'em a long way off. When I was stumbling around your ruined towns, overgrown fields, it gave me something to shoot for."

Targ's mouth was open; he was hanging on my every word. "And what did you hope to find here, Siscoe?"

"Civilization."

"Yes . . . and *then*?"

"A transmitter, Targ, to get me off this world. What else?"

Targ let out his breath. "Of course, Siscoe, a transmitter. What else, indeed."

They were all staring at me, the girl, Casparian, the old geezer; no one moved, as if the scene had been frozen solid.

Targ broke the silence, his voice a mere raspy whisper. "And where, Siscoe, is the transmitter located?"

"That's what I was going to ask you, pal."

Targ's face turned beet-red; his little eyes tried to burn holes into me. *"You don't know?"*

"How the hell am I supposed to know? I didn't even know this world existed till I got here."

Targ sank back in his chair, his face going from red to ashen white; he seemed to shrivel up right before me as though he'd aged another decade or so. "He doesn't know," he croaked.

"Well, well, it was a slim chance at best." Casparian sighed.

"We have waited so long," Targ whispered.

"We'll wait some more, that's all," Rava said.

"Easy for you," Targ said. "I will never live to see the day."

"What's the problem?" I asked.

"Nothing you can help with," Targ said.

"Possibly. Try me. What've you got to lose?"

"We," Casparian said, "are completely isolated, on the very edge of the universe one might say. No more than a dozen manned ships have reached us during the last thousand years. These have added greatly to our well-being, have acquainted us with the many marvels which exist in the greater universe, the myriad worlds and cultures. We owe much of our technical progress, and even a good deal of our culture, to these ambassadors."

"Bah," Targ said. "What Casparian means is that these ships only whetted our appetite, showed us how cut-off we were."

"How long," I asked, "does it take a spaceship to get here?"

"More than a century," Rava said.

"Yeah, I can see why you folks might get a bit impatient."

"The ships came on automatic," Casparian said. "The pilot and passengers slept through the greater part of the journey. What they brought us was of necessity a hundred years old."

"Out of date!" Targ snapped. "Industry on Xcroth is centuries behind the times."

"Not in the Secret Police building it isn't," I said. "You boys are right in step with your spotter eyes, magento-ears, monitors, and computers. Makes an old ex-con like me feel right at home."

"Ex-convict?" Casparian said.

I shrugged. "Trumped-up charges."

"Political?" Casparian asked.

"Sure."

"Those innovations are what first attracted our attention," Casparian said.

"The military and the Secret Police were first," Rava said. "They came up with things no one else had, or even knew what to do with. And they kept it for themselves. It's all classified. Our experts said it was too advanced to be the product of our home-grown scientists. We thought at first they'd gotten hold of a new spaceship, put it under wraps. But the rumor didn't check out. That was years ago. Before the war split the globe into two camps. Things are worse now. The military and their helpers run everything. Much more is classified. The standard of living goes down each year—"

"Bad for business," Targ snapped.

"Doesn't sound too hot for anything else either," I said.

Targ said, "The Power, Siscoe, is an amalgam of the military, various police systems, selected manufacturers, and assorted politicians. They are on one side. Everyone else is on the other. And the Power is being aided and abetted by offworlders."

"Through a transmitter?" I said.

"That," Targ said, "is what we believe."

"The grapevine has long hinted at such a device," Casprian said. "I joined the Secret Police solely to seek it out. But I must confess I have made absolutely no progress in finding one during my years on the force."

"And you're one of their top guys?" I said.

"I was," Casparian said glumly, "until now."

"Sorry about that," I said.

"An outcast, one of the wasteland inhabitants," Rava said, "gave us our first clue."

"Us?" I said.

"We are the Fellowship," Targ said.

"I thought you were the Manufacturers' Guild."

"That too, Siscoe."

"So what's this Fellowship?"

"An outlaw group," Casparian said.

"Crooks?"

"There are times when it takes crooks to beat crooks." Targ grinned. "Or merely to survive."

"You boys go around spilling the beans to strangers?"

"Only when they are offworlders," Targ said, "and hunted by the Power. That makes them even bigger crooks than we are."

"And your outcasts?" I said.

"They're former citizens," Rava said, "who, for one reason or another, have had a run-in with the Power."

I said, "They don't look too scrappy to me."

"Not anymore," Rava said. "They've undergone the treatment."

"They serve as object lessons," Casparian said. "They are put out in the wastelands to perish. And in their reduced state, that is precisely what they do! And if not, they are helped along by the wasteland scouts, the strike force."

"The blue boys?"

Casparian nodded.

"The Fellowship's contacts are even among the

outcasts," Rava said. "We help them whenever we can. They alerted us."

I grinned at her. "Told you some guy had come popping out of that house, right?"

"You *knew*?" Rava said.

"What knew? If I could come calling that way, so could someone else."

"It's the metal platform," she said, "isn't it?"

"Yeah, that's what it is."

"But it appears to be dismantled," Casparian said.

"Right again. It's a one-way ticket to here."

"And it cannot be repaired?" Targ asked.

"Why bother," I said, "when we can build a new one?"

The three of them turned to stare at me as if I'd just sprouted a pair of antlers.

"I beg your pardon," Targ said.

"Make a new one," I said.

"You are a *scientist*?" Casparian asked.

"That and a couple of other things. On my off days."

"Siscoe," Targ said, "am I to understand that you actually carry the plans of this transmitter . . . in your head?"

"Yeah, that's what you're to understand."

"It is common knowledge out in the galaxy?"

"I wouldn't say that."

"Do all who use a transmitter know how to construct one?"

"I wouldn't say that either."

"What *would* you say?"

"Maybe two guys in the whole universe know how to build one of those babies, Targ, and you're speaking to one of 'em."

Targ's mouth opened, closed. "I do not know what to say," he said.

" 'Thanks' might do for starters," I told him.

"Frankly, I find it incredible."

"Don't you find it a bit strange too that I speak your language?"

"Yes, now that you mention it."

I tapped my noodle with a knuckle. "I learned it. On the spot, pal."

"How, Siscoe?"

"Put together a trio of antique lingos that your visitors must've brought along during the last thousand years. And you folks adopted as your own."

"Yes," Targ said, "they were the rage, our historians tell us. That was well over seven hundred years ago. There have been some changes in Xcroth since then."

"I'm sure."

Targ leaned forward. "And how did you master those?"

"Mnemonic adapter, triggered by an autohypno code word." I grinned at him. "Got a hundred more lingos bouncing around my skull, too. And more facts and figures about the universe than I could ever tell you. The transmitter is one of those. And it's yours for the asking."

"But how did you come by this knowledge?" Targ asked. "How could you absorb it all?"

"Out there in the universe, there's a guy who runs the show; he's called the Chairman. His scientists found a way to expand the mind. I got to use the process. It's that simple."

Rava said, "What if you're lying?"

"Why should I do that?" I asked reasonably enough.

Rava shrugged a slim shoulder. "Why should you do *anything*? You're an offworlder. Your motives might very well be beyond our grasp. Or you might be a spy from the Power. Or a Ludie. Planted in that house to deceive us."

"Yeah," I admitted, "I might. But there's one way to find out, isn't there?"

"And what would that be?" Casparian asked.

"Easy. Have Worts take a peek in my bean."

"Our Worts is not always accurate," Casparian said.

"But he's not always wrong either. And, of course, I could just go ahead and build the damn contraption. That'd be the clincher, all right. What've you got to lose?"

"Nothing," Targ said. His eyes lit up. "And everything to gain."

"Couldn't've put it better myself," I said.

"What is it you'll need?" Targ asked.

I settled back in my chair, folded my arms across my chest, and began to tell him.

A couple of hours had dragged by. Down below, the streets were bustling again, pedestrians and bubbletops clogging the main arteries. The men in green were gone, the alert over.

And since I was still on the loose the Power would have to chalk up its Ludie hunt as a dud. At least for now. That was dandy with me.

I looked at Casparian. He didn't seem any too chipper. I said, "Think they're on to you yet?"

The fat man mopped his brow with a polka-dot hanky, grinned at me. "Absolutely." His face seemed a bit yellow around the edges.

"But you're taking it in stride."

He shrugged. "I have made preparations for such a contingency. An alternate identity, a modest cottage on the outskirts of town, a good deal of credit salted away."

"Sounds cozy."

He sighed. "It will do me no good. Sooner or later they will find me. The Power knows no limits, reaches into all walks of life. I am, as the saying goes, a hopeless case."

"That's the saying, all right," I said.

Casparian shrugged. "It is to be expected. A double role such as I have played is always a perilous undertaking."

"Then why bother?"

"The times demand it."

Rava said, "Siscoe's great mind doesn't seem to include a knowledge of current history."

"Don't expect miracles, lady."

"The Power is all-pervasive," Casparian said. "Its stranglehold on the economy, on industry, on technology has had dire consequences. We are dying."

"They don't know that?"

"They are fanatics. A harsh, puritanical ethic binds the land. Duty is the watchword. Numerous grades of citizens abound. The lesser categories are exiled to the gray towns, where they labor endlessly in factories."

"No automation?"

"The word is unknown except to the higher echelons. Yes, Siscoe, automation exists on Xcroth. But only in the armaments industry. And that is a Power monopoly. The term is classified. Along with many other scientific advances which never reach the public. The Power supports the most conservative institutions. The cults, the castes, the guilds. The results are overpopulation—birth control is a crime—slums, poverty. Each year we sink deeper into this morass."

"You folks've really got a swell setup," I said.

"No worse than the North."

"What's the system there?"

"Why, it is almost identical to ours."

"Then what's the beef?"

"It's about a slice of land," Rava said. "It's almost all sand. We have half, they have half. No one lives there, nothing can grow there. Both sides want all of it."

"Sounds reasonable enough," I said. "That's the way they do things on lots of worlds."

"Really?" Rava said.

"Sure. What's left of them. Any big wars yet?"

"Only skirmishes," Casparian said, "some major, some minor. The wastelands are the result."

"You boys saving your Sunday punch for a rainy day, or just showing lots of restraint?"

Casparian laughed. "Hardly restraint. Terror weapons maintain the peace, such as it is: x-bombs, death vapors, plague capsules."

"Big-league stuff," I told him.

"Their use would mean the end of life on Xcroth. It is this 'emergency' that justifies martial law, that allows the Power to continue its insane rule."

I said, "Kind of tough on the citizens."

"There is wholesale despair," Casparian said.

"Licensed euphorics take some of the edge off," Rava said.

"Outbreaks of sudden violence are commonplace," Casparian said.

"Just a laugh a minute," I said.

"But with a transmitter," Casparian said, "there would be hope again. We could reach out for help."

"The transmitter's a two-way street," I said. "You might get more than you bargained for."

"We'll take our chances," Rava said.

Targ stepped back into the room, closed the hall door behind him, shuffled over to his armchair, sank into it with a sigh.

"It won't do, Siscoe," Targ said.

"No, huh?"

"I have run your list of materials through our computer—"

"What computer?"

"The Fellowship's."

"Here?"

"Don't be inane, Siscoe. It is quite well hidden. But if one knows the code, it is a simple matter to punch out the proper digits on the communo and plug into the set."

"And you've done that."

"Indeed I have. But the results were hardly gratifying. Fully one-third of the items you requested are classified, directly controlled by the Power. They are used in the armaments industry."

"No ins there?" I asked.

"A nodding acquaintance with some of the directors, perhaps."

"As long as we can get a foot in the door," I said. "What about the other two-thirds?"

"They are available in one form or another. We can beg, borrow, or steal. And in some cases we can even purchase the products."

"You have the funds?"

"The Fellowship, Siscoe, consists of numerous businessmen who have discovered to their dismay that the Power is bad for business. Many of their transactions now occur ouside the official economic structure. The Fellowship is instrumental in developing such unofficial channels. And is paid five percent for its efforts."

I said, "We're talking about the black market, huh?"

"Of course."

"Then you must have part of the underworld in your pocket too."

Targ leaned back in his chair, smiled sweetly at me. "Our organization, Siscoe, in many ways *is* the underworld."

"I'm talking about bank stickups, loansharking, the protection racket, that sort of underworld."

Targ nodded pleasantly. "So am I."

"Well, well," I said.

"Given the scope of the Power, Siscoe, its all-pervasive character, an alliance between the under-world and business makes perfect sense. It is plainly in both our interests to work together."

"Not bad. We're going to need some strongarm help before this is over."

"I'm sure that can be arranged," Targ said. "Is there anything else you require?"

"You'll take care of the aboveboard materials?" I asked.

"I am permitted to draw on Fellowship funds. For special projects. I have, in fact, unlimited access."

"Can't ask for more than that," I said. "Leaving the one-third the Power's sitting on. I'll need some help prying that loose. Who runs your underworld operation here?"

"Jilks."

"Good. I'd like to meet him. Sooner the better."

"That can be arranged."

"I'll need a computer printout of which outfits have the classified items, where they're located, who heads 'em up."

"That is no problem," Targ said. "With one small exception."

"Yeah?"

"The fuel pile."

"What about it?"

"We have it. But not the Q-enriched product. Our scientists here in the south seem to have lagged in this respect. But they are on the verge of perfecting the processes. Three more years perhaps, five at the most, and the plants necessary to produce the Q enrichment will be completed."

"Too long," I told him.

"The product *is* available in the North, Siscoe."

"That's more like it. How can I get there?"

"With great difficulty," Targ said. "There is no legal commerce between North and South. The North, however, harbors a syndicate very much like our own called the Brotherhood. We have our contacts."

"You'll use them?"

"To help build the transmitter? What do *you* think, Siscoe?"

CHAPTER
15

Block had forgotten how hard finding a parking space could be in SoHo, even on a weeknight. Ten minutes of driving finally produced one.

He locked the car door, walked off into the bustling streets carrying his two briefcases under one arm and the small trunk under the other. By the time he reached Spring Street and West Broadway he was starting to feel tired.

The lights were on in Nora's flat. He stood on the corner across the street and tried to wash out the memory of this last year, to return somehow to a simpler, less hectic version of himself. He didn't succeed.

Block crossed over, rang the bell, identified himself for the intercom, was buzzed in, and walked up two flights of stairs to apartment 3D, his second home.

She was waiting for him at the door. Her face was oval, nose pert, lips thin, eyes large and dark brown. Curly light brown hair fell over her shoulders. She had on a greenish-gray cashmere sweater, a red-and-black-checked skirt. She was twenty-eight, but the hallway's dim light reduced her years, made her a teenager again.

"You said you wouldn't come."

"I lied," he told her.

The embrace didn't work too well until Block unloaded his baggage inside. It worked fine after that.

"More coffee?"

"Sure."

She poured, put the coffee pot back on the end table, curled up against him on the couch.

"Okay," she said, "talk."

"Well," he said, "there's no way for me to prove that Charles Hastings killed Marty Nash. None. But Hastings was a busy lad. Had lots of irons in the fire."

"And you're checking into them all."

"See? You know the answers already," Block said.

"Hastings was responsible for your memory lapse."

"Uh-huh."

"What makes you think, Ross, that this time he won't do *more* than just make you forget?"

"Like what?"

"Kill you."

"Because I've got him on the run, sweetie. He's powdered out. Gave up his business and everything."

"And you'll track him down."

"Sooner or later. I've been nosing around the McCoy establishment. Came up with lots of goodies. Gotta sort them out first."

"But why, Ross? Haven't you done *enough*?"

"More than enough."

"So?"

"So I've got to come up with *something*, My disappearing act, stint on the Bowery, year's absence without leave. All that didn't go over too well at the paper. A big story would take care of that."

"And *that's* why you're doing all this?"

"Reason enough."

"It's hateful, Ross."

He sighed. "Funny you should say that."

Block rolled quietly off the bed. Nora was sleeping peacefully on her side. He left her that way, tiptoed out into the living room, closing the bedroom door behind him.

The clock said 2:25.

He put on his robe and slippers, went to the window, glanced down at a darkened Soho. A lone figure weaved its way across the empty pavement, having obviously hit one bar too many. Stores had doused their show windows for the night. Only a couple of cars cruised by as he watched. Streetlamps cast a frozen glare into the dark. The few sounds there were seemed to come from somewhere over the rooftops.

Block looked up at the sky. A handful of stars could be seen. The Control World was out there, along with the hundreds of worlds making up the Galactic Arm. He knew it, but could hardly believe it himself. No one would believe him if he told them, no one except Pabst.

Block shivered, tightened the robe's belt around him, turned from the window, and got to work.

He seated himself at the kitchen table, used a screwdriver to dismantle the lock on Pavel's trunk. It was stuffed with documents, all relating to McCoy.

He snapped open the pair of briefcases he'd wangled from Ben Cohen. His colleagues, he saw, had done themselves proud snooping into the affairs of Nash, Siscoe, and the McCoy enterprise. Siscoe he had down pat, his memory tape lodged firmly in his mind. But the rest of this stuff looked promising.

He rose, went to the hall closet, rummaged in a jacket pocket, came up with Draden's list of McCoy personnel and operations, carried it back to the table.

Block made neat piles of all the material on the

table top, leaned back on his hard kitchen chair, and surveyed it gloomily. A staff of trained investigators would have had no trouble going through this stuff in a couple of days and making some sense of it. It wasn't Block's kind of job.

Fortunately, he wasn't quite without an angle.

Pabst had run the show on Earth. His reports to the Chairman had been short on detail, of a general nature. But what information the Chairman had been given, he now had stuck in his mind.

That made things smoother.

Block activated the Chairman's autohypno code, stacked Pabst's data in a corner of his mind where he could measure it against his other findings.

A second code set up the Chairman's mnemonic system. A third shifted the entire operation to his unconscious.

He was ready.

Block's hand reached for the nearest sheaf of papers. He started turning pages.

The sky grew lighter outside.

He laid down the last sheet, sat back in his chair, rubbed his eyes. He was beat, ready for another five-hour session on the mattress. But he knew a little more now than when he'd begun. Uncovering the Pabst network didn't seem quite so hard anymore.

He repacked his data, stood up, stretched, yawned, tiptoed back into the bedroom.

Nora was still in slumberland.

He crawled in under the sheets next to her, closed his eyes, and went to sleep. He dreamed of crooked business deals.

CHAPTER

16

"That's idiotic," Jilks said.

"There, there," Casparian said, waving his arm as if trying to smooth out wrinkles on an invisible suit.

I got up from the sofa, strolled to a window, and pushed aside the drapes. Bright lights in tall buildings twinkled at me through the darkness.

"You really expect me to give an offworlder the run of my outfit?" Jilks was saying behind me.

"*Our* outfit," Casparian said. "You should not forget that salient point."

"You're crazy," Jilks said.

The quarrel had been going on now for a couple of hours. This Jilks was a small, soft-looking bird somewhere in his fifties. His face was round, eyes hazel and heavy-lidded, hair dark and slicked back. A trim mustache decorated his upper lip. He wore a belted maroon dressing gown and yellow house slippers. If this guy was a crime czar, I was a three-legged barstool. On the other hand, who could tell what a crime czar was on this backwater world? Jilks's digs didn't do much for his image either. We were high up in a penthouse, a half-dozen miles from the white government buildings. Houses around us were slim, streamlined affairs; the Jilks suite was plush and luxurious. If nothing else, it proved that crime paid plenty on Xcroth, just as it did everywhere else. I turned, leaned up against the sill, took in the show.

Casparian said, "You are being quite unreasonable, Jilks. This man can open new worlds for us, change the quality of life on the entire planet."

Jilks looked disgusted. "Who wants change?"

Rava said, "You've sponged off the Committee, Jilks. We've set you up lots of times, given you the data to pull one job after another. Our commission is small for so much profit."

Jilks shrugged. "I don't make the rules," he said. "If you've got a grievance, take it up with the Council."

Rava said, "That's exactly what I plan to do."

"It is absolutely essential that our request be carried out promptly," Casparian said.

Jilks grinned sourly. "Even if I gave you the go-ahead, what makes you think the boys would go along with this? What's in it for them? They've got to take a lot of senseless risks for some big future payoff. And all on the say-so of a stranger. The whole thing's a joke."

"The transmitter," Casparian said, "is worth any risk."

"What transmitter?" Jilks said. "You really believe in that old wives' tale?"

"He was seen stepping out of the house," Rava said.

"Could've gotten in the back way," Jilks said.

"He didn't," she said.

Jilks turned, gave me a long, hard look. "Speaks the language like a native, doesn't he?"

"We've explained that," Rava said.

"Some explanation," Jilks said.

"We see it as proof," Casparian said.

"Great proof," Jilks said.

"The responsibility rests with us," Casparian said.

"A lot of good that will do," Jilks said, "if he sinks us all."

"No one's going to sink anything," I said, "I'm not asking for a blank check. I'm willing to funnel everything through you, Jilks. If it's not sound, if you've got any complaints, we scrap it, start over. What could be simpler?"

Jilks said, "Your going back where you came from."

"I wish I could, pal. Gimme a hand and maybe we can swing it. Meanwhile, there's plenty of profit here for everyone. I've got a couple of angles, well tested on a dozen worlds, that ought to see us both in clover."

"Save it, offworlder. We're doing fine without your help," Jilks said.

"This will go to the Council," Casparian said.

"Anything you want," Jilks said. "Just go and take him with you."

"You'll regret this," Casparian said.

"Not half as much as if I'd joined you in this hare-brained scheme," Jilks said.

Darkness had spilled over the streets. From inside the bubbletop, I got only a fleeting glimpse of the neighborhoods we rode through. Streetlamps were far apart in what I took to be the outlying reaches of the Hub. There were no lights at all on the highway.

Casparian was at the wheel. He said, "I wouldn't worry too much about Jilks. The Council will come down on your side."

"How can you be so sure?" I asked.

"We've got the votes," Rava said.

"Yes, indeed," Casparian said. "The Council is made up of various Fellowship constituents. Both those aboveboard and those outside the law. Criminals, in short. Jilks is spokesman for a significant segment of the criminal community. But hardly for all of it. His is but one vote on the Council. We have bought some of the others, enough to ensure the proper outcome."

"So I'm in business?"

"It's not that simple, Siscoe," Rava said.

"Never is," I said.

"Jilks is no pushover," she said. "He could get in the way."

"We will have to neutralize him," Casparian said.

"Can you?" I asked.

The fat man shrugged. "Nothing is certain."

We left the highway, turned down a narrow bumpy road; sand dunes seemed to be on the right and left of us. Soon we were racing along parallel to a large body of water.

"Vacation spot?" I asked.

"For some," Casparian said.

"And for me?"

"A house where no one will find you," Rava said.

"I wouldn't mind," I said, "all things considered. But I'm kind of anxious to get back into circulation. You've got a nice world here—"

"Stinks," Rava said.

"Yeah. But it beats the prison world I used to call home. Thing is, I gotta get back to where I came from. The sooner the better."

"Things are happening there?" Casparian asked.

"You could say that."

"Well, we must be patient," Casparian said.

"For how long?"

"We must create an identity for you," Casparian said. "The necessary documents can be either purchased or forged. That is easy enough."

"But we can't have you traipsing around," Rava said, "when you don't know your left foot from your right."

"I'm stupid," I admitted, "but if I kept my mind

on it, I could probably figure out which was which."

"True," Rava said, "but I can help. You a quick study?"

"The quickest."

"Good. While we wait for the Council to meet, for your identity to take shape, we'll study."

"And then?"

"You'll give them hell."

Waves beat against the shore. The sound woke me. I rolled out of bed. My nightstand was piled high with folders, books, journals. I looked at them glumly. They were all about Xcroth. Others were scattered all through the house, possibly five hundred items in all. I'd gone through most of them, using the Chairman's autohypno key to fix them in my mind. I'd studied street maps, volumes of who's whos in anything that seemed to matter, and a lot that didn't. I'd skimmed the scientific literature hunting for anything that might help build a transmitter. I'd sharpened my language skill to a fine cutting edge. Rava had brought the material, one load after another, and I'd gone through the lot. Five days had crept by, not the most inspiring ones I could remember, and by now I knew all about Xcroth, probably a bit more than its leading citizens knew or wanted to know. And my one overriding desire was to get off the planet.

Rava said, "Got it down pat yet?"

"I'm a walking encyclopedia."

"Good. Today's the day. You become Kall the Battler."

"Kall? You couldn't come up with a better name?"

"There really was a Kall," Rava said. "That's an advantage."

"What happened to him?" I asked.

"He died. Of wounds sustained in a bout." She looked at me. "This was your idea. I hope you know what you're doing."

"Don't worry about me," I said with more confidence than I felt. "You just hold up your end."

She passed me a large envelope. I emptied it out on the table. An ID. An internal passport that would get me around the country. A second-class citizen certificate. A folder detailing Kall's history. A picture came with the folder. Kall was a big bruiser, with a busted nose, large lips, and a cauliflower ear.

"No one's going to take me for this lug," I complained. "You folks crazy?"

"Relax, Siscoe. Kall fought wearing a mask. He came from a small town in the northeast that isn't even on the map. And he never got much beyond the provincial capital. He's made to order for you."

"Okay," I said. "What about Jilks?"

Rava smiled. "The vote went against him."

"That'll hold him?"

She shrugged. "He's too smart to make trouble."

"You sure?"

"No."

I could hear the crowd's roar from my dressing room.

The door opened. A guy who needed a shave stuck his head in. "You're next, bud."

I put the mask over my head. "Come on, Worts," I said.

Worts mopped his brow. "I'm not at all sure this will work."

"You feel okay?" I asked him. A funny enough question, since I was the sucker headed for the ring. But an important one.

"I think so."

"That's all that matters."

*   *   *

I sat on my stool and looked across the ring. The guy I was going to fight—Zag the Basher—wasn't the biggest guy I'd ever seen. I'd seen maybe ten or twelve who were even bigger. There was small comfort in that fact. He had close-cropped black hair, muscles on his muscles, a flattened nose, and lots of scars to prove he'd been in a tussle or two. If anyone still needed proof after taking a glance at him. He was glaring at me. The guy looked as though he meant business.

The pair of guards in the ring with us were ready for anything. They had their long pointy spears, their nets, their electrical prod sticks. If one of the gladiators was killing the other and wouldn't stop, the guards would try to separate them. Sometimes they even did, word had it.

The crowd made plenty of noise. The stadium was packed. Zag the Basher was probably going to grind me into small bits and pieces and feed me to the birds. But this crowd had come to see me, not him. The first fifty rows were filled with the Hub's top citizens, the next fifty with those who aspired to the top. The appearance of Kall the Battler in their midst had brought them out in droves. I was an instant celebrity, helped along by all the hoopla the Fellowship could bring into play and then some.

The Fellowship had pulled all the stops to put me on the map. They had a number of media bigwigs as members—and a lot more running errands—and these birds got busy blowing my horn; they blew long and hard. My masked face was plastered all over town on posters and billboards. I'd been written up in the sports pages of all the dailies, interviewed on the audio, made the news views in the pleasure palaces.

The gladiator game was under the crime syndicate's thumb. Putting the match together had been a snap.

They were billing me as the next champ. The fix was in too, so I had nothing to worry about. Only I was worried.

Worts was in my corner. He was sweating. He leaned over the ropes, whispered in my ear, "It's a double cross."

"That's what I figured," I told him.

"He's going to rush you."

"Thanks. Get set to do your stuff."

"But I am not—"

"Too late for buts, pal," I told him.

The beeper beeped.

I was up on my feet.

I'd worked out plenty these last few weeks. I'd used the autohypno key to make me a tiger, sifted through the Chairman's mind to get the lowdown on all the strong arm tapes he'd fed himself. And back on Earth I'd once been a boxer. But there was no use kidding myself. I was way past my prime. Middle age and a stint on the penal world had done nothing for my stamina. The fix was supposed to put me over. But the fix was dead and buried. Leaving just me and Worts. I wondered if the pair of us had a chance.

The horn sounded.

Time to go. I took only about eight steps.

Zag launched himself at me. He didn't look much bigger than a tank. He was fast. He'd have rolled right over me if Worts hadn't tipped me to this move.

The surprise on my face must have encouraged Zag. His hands reached for me.

I stepped aside, sliced down hard on Zag's neck as he sailed past me into the ropes.

Zag turned and sprang at me again in one motion. Some Zag.

I fell flat to the canvas and Zag flew over me.

I scrambled to my feet in time to see Zag charge again.

This Zag was going to be a problem. I couldn't keep dodging him all night. But if I ever got close enough to grapple with him, he'd probably pull me apart piece by piece.

I tapped the judo autohypno key.

Zag put a meaty hand on my shoulder. I got hold of his forearm and elbow. All on its own my body twisted sideways, my hands pulled. Zag shot into the ring post, bounced to the canvas, bounced up, and landed a roundhouse right to my chest.

I went backward as though a cannon ball had collided with me. The ropes at my back stopped me. I went down on my knees, rolled over on my back. The crowd roared. The lights overhead took to whirling around; they blinked on and off. A voice in my ear was saying, "Out of your league, Siscoe." That voice, which was mine, spoke wisdom.

Zag was busy posturing for the crowd, flexing his muscles. I looked out for the count. Only here, on Xcroth, there was no count. The only way out of the ring was on a stretcher.

I used the autohypno key, and the ring stopped spinning. I used a second key and felt almost whole again. Almost wasn't going to last long, I knew, not when Zag got through with me.

It was now or never.

Zag had seen me move. That got his attention. Next instant Zag was an object that came hurtling at me through the air.

I brought my legs back, released them with a snap. My feet struck his chest. He went bouncing off in the other direction.

He didn't bounce very far.

Zag glowered at me, annoyance plain on his face. By now I should have been dead to the world, but here I was still showing signs of life. Zag would fix that.

I had no doubt that he could.

He started moving toward me slowly.

I climbed to my feet. It wasn't all that easy.

This time Zag wasn't going to rush me. He was going to take his time and do the job right. Zag was going to kill me.

The crowd sensed it, began to scream.

At the start they'd all been on my side, anxious to see the masked stranger make his mark. Now the tide had turned. This crowd wanted blood. And I seemed the most likely candidate.

I was up against the ropes, near one corner. There was no place to run.

Zag took another step.

I jerked a thumb up in the air, gave Worts the high sign.

Worts closed his eyes, leaned against the ring apron.

Zag took a final step. I was in range now. He raised a fist, ready to smash in my face. And he let it hang there like a balloon floating next to his head. His eyes widened, blinked; there was fear in them. Zag seemed to forget all about me. He swayed, gripped by the same terror, the same churning whirlpool that had engulfed me when Worts had done his stuff, made his first contact.

I managed to land a right jab and left cross before Zag tumbled to the canvas.

The crowd was on its feet screaming, "Kall, Kall!" So they must have bought it.

I kicked Zag a couple of times to show he was out of it. The fallen gladiator just twitched, lay there moaning, his eyes wild. He wasn't getting up. The whirlpool had knocked him for a loop—just as it had me.

The pair of guards raised their spears, signaling victory. Mine.

I held up my hands toward the screaming crowd. My thumb and forefinger plucked the mask from my face. The crowd cheered. From here on in, I would be a recognizable celebrity, someone the cops would bother only for his autograph.

I glanced over at Worts.

His face glistened with sweat. His eyes were still tightly closed.

As I watched, Worts slowly slipped from view, vanished somewhere below the ring, on the floorboards. The little guy had passed out cold.

Zag's eyes focused suddenly. He looked around as if wondering what he was doing stretched out on the canvas.

Before Zag figured out he had a grievance, I climbed through the ropes, picked Worts off the floor, and with the crowd closing in all around me, made my way as fast as I could back to the dressing room.

"Jilks."

"Siscoe."

"I'd like a word with you."

The short man shrugged, stepped back from the door. We went into the living room.

"Good fight," Jilks said.

"Thanks."

"Looked a bit shaky at first."

"Looked isn't the half of it."

"But you pulled it off, Siscoe, kid."

"Yeah. No thanks to you, Jilks."

"I don't believe I quite understand."

"Sure you do."

"Perhaps you had better enlighten me."

"The fight was fixed."

"Tsk, tsk."

"Yeah. But the fix came undone."

"You don't say?"

"But I do, Jilks. And I almost got my head handed to me."

"You won, though."

"By a whisker."

"Still—" He shrugged.

"Listen, Jilks, I wasn't after a title or purse. I've got enough of both where I come from. This thing was a setup, a way for me to make the right contacts, get to the right places, start work on a transmitter. The plan had the Council's backing."

"The vote was rigged."

"That's not my problem, pal; I don't make the rules around here."

"What is your problem?"

"You."

"Yes?"

"Getting you out of my hair."

Jilks shrugged. "You really believe I bought off your opponent?"

"Yeah."

"Why?"

"Worts."

"Our so-called mind reader?"

"That's the guy."

"He probed my mind."

"Not you, pal. Zag."

"Zag."

I nodded. "Guy was under the impression the credit came from you."

"Impression."

"So the go-between said."

"This go-between, he has a name?"

"Worts didn't get that."

Jilks smiled. "Not much of a case, is there?"

"Who cares about cases?"

"You."

"Forget that."

"Very generous."

"Live and let live."

"That's what you came to tell me?"

"Yeah. Along with this. If I'm fingered, I'll know who did it. And I'll know who to come looking for. So will the Fellowship. That clear?"

"Abundantly."

"Glad to hear it. That was the bad news."

"There's good?"

"Sure. Building the transmitter is going to take some credit."

"I don't believe in this transmitter of yours."

"Doesn't matter. You believe in credit, don't you?"

"Certainly."

"Well, there's going to be plenty going around. Behave yourself and you'll get rich."

"I am rich."

"You'll get richer."

Targ said, "You have seen Kall in action, have you not?"

"Oh, the Battler. Of course." The heavyset, white-haired man snapped his heels in greeting. I snapped mine. It was very chummy. Around us the party buzzed and bubbled. The top-drawer Hub manufacturing moguls were on display here. Their costumes were a rainbow of colors. Tables were piled high with delicacies, euphorics, regeneratives. Happy powder was sniffed, tasted, injected. Music came from the fifty-piece orchestra by the swimming pool. Overhead the penthouse bubble dome held back the night. Stars glittered out there. But probably no more than sauntered through this giant room.

"Balk here," Targ said, "is the leading electronics manufacturer in the Hub."

Balk denied it. "In the whole of South Xcroth." He beamed.

Targ lowered his voice. "Kall is anxious to invest some credits."

"Really?" Balk said.

"If the returns are adequate, of course," Targ said.

"Of course," Balk said. "A small investment, no doubt?"

"On the contrary," Targ said, "Kall's fortune is quite substantial."

"Fortune?"

"I've got a bit put away," I told him modestly.

"Well, well."

"Electronics," I said, "has always interested me."

"I told him he couldn't go far wrong if he bought into your firm," Targ said.

"True," Balk said.

"Thought you might give him the tour," Targ said.

"The plant?" Balk said.

"No," Targ said.

"The generator?"

Targ shook his head.

"The laboratory, then?"

"Sounds interesting," I said.

"An excellent choice," Targ beamed.

"We'll show you an item or two, Kall, that will open your eyes."

Targ and I moved on.

I said, "If that guy's so rich, how come he needs investors?"

"He's not so rich," Targ said. "And he's greedy. They all are." His hand swept the room. "We're counting on that."

We went from one group to the next. The music grew louder, the crowd more raucous. I met other bigwigs, gave them my spiel.

After a while I got Targ off in a corner. "Some of

these babies are going to check out my story," I told
him.

"I certainly hope so," Targ said.

"This Kall was loaded?"

"He had a weak spot for the gaming tables. What
little he earned in the ring went to them."

"Great. Where does that leave me?"

Targ grinned. "With a sizable fortune."

"I won a jackpot?"

"You had a shrewd investment counselor. His name
was Delph. You might recommend him to others."

"One of you guys?"

"Naturally. It has all been taken care of. An account
was registered in your name. I personally transferred
the funds."

"Thanks."

"A small price to pay for a transmitter."

It took about a week.

Kall the Battler without credit would have been a
mere curiosity, one soon forgotten. Kall the investor
was something else. The Xcroth economy was nothing to brag about, had been on a downswing for close
to a decade. Investors were given the royal treatment.
I was wined, dined, and taken on the grand tour.

The tour was the interesting part.

Kall the Battler wouldn't have known a magno-
tube from a hole in the wall. Nick Siscoe, Earthman,
was no whiz either. But the guy with the Chairman's
mind in tow was a real world beater.

I was ushered into gleaming labs, giant steelworks,
assembly plants, hardware and software factories.
The autohypno key kept clicking away, taking mental snapshots. I smiled, nodded, looked impressed. I
was.

The red carpet worked wonders, even got me
through locked doors. Some of the outfits I visited

did chores for the military. Off limits for civilians. But Kall the Battler was different. Besides being a credit czar, this Kall was a celeb and hardly trained in technology. I got an eyeful. Not all the spots I wanted to visit. But enough.

A wind was blowing. The sky was slate-gray. Bluish mountains were on all sides of us.

I pulled my hat low, stuck my hands into the pockets of my ankle-length coat. And shivered.

Casparian beamed at me. "What do you think?"

"It's big enough."

"Wait until you see the inside."

We left our two-seater copter, moved toward the three-level structure.

"We built it here."

"The Fellowship?"

"Its scientific arm."

"Jilks knows?"

"Hardly his concern."

"Glad to hear it."

Inside was a buzz of activity. Blue-clad techs scurried around; men and women worked at long metal tables. Machines hummed in the background.

"Almost like home," I told Casparian. "Except for the foreman and union rep."

The fat man wobbled his chins at me. "Those who work here consider it a privilege. They are helping to build the new order."

"How long they been at it?"

"Five years."

"Slow going."

"It will speed up now that you are here."

"Where's our project?"

"Second level."

"Let see what's to see."

Upstairs was deserted. A large metal scaffold had

been constructed. Wire coils, parts of machinery stuck out. I spent some twenty minutes checking crates, going over blueprints, working my way down a long inventory list.

"About two-thirds done," I told Casparian.

He nodded. "We can go no further without the classified material."

"And that's at?"

"Our friend Balk's laboratories. The Military Research Center. The physics complex. A half-dozen others."

"Sounds simple enough."

"Allow me to inform you," Casparian said. "These sites are the most closely guarded. The most advanced devices are in use. As a former member of our Secret Police, I can assure you that there is almost no hope of penetrating these areas."

"You said almost."

"Yes."

"Good. I'm going to draw up some blueprints for your crew here to work on. I'll want this stuff on the double. And then I'd like you to introduce me to a couple of your crime chiefs."

"Jilks will find out."

"He's going to blow the whistle on his own boys?"

"Not if he wishes to survive."

"Okay. We'll take the chance."

"What are you planning?"

"A crime wave."

CHAPTER
17

The smell of perking coffee woke him.

He got out of bed, padded through the living room, waved hi to Nora, who was busy in the kitchen, went into the bathroom, and washed up.

Breakfast was scrambled eggs, bacon, wheat toast, orange marmalade, and three cups of coffee. They ate at the kitchen table.

Nora said, "You were up last night."

"Woke you, eh?"

"Bedsprings creaked."

He took a bite of toast, a swallow of coffee. "Dead giveaway."

"Insomnia?"

"Paperwork."

"McCoy?"

"Sure. All about McCoy. Tons of junk. Looks like nothing at first. Takes a shrewd eye to detect anything. But after a while the papers start to connect. A devious picture begins to emerge. I wonder, am I making sense?"

"Not much."

"Listen. The question is: Why would Hastings up and fold McCoy, and lose his shirt in the bargain?"

"Why?"

"That's right, why. Because he's got something bigger, better, on the fire."

"Sounds reasonable."

"What Hastings has is a thing called World-Wide."

"What?"

"They manufacture computer parts, sweetie."

"Doesn't *everyone*?"

"Maybe. But World-Wide really *is* worldwide. Makes a difference."

"Like a *household* name, you mean."

"Not quite. Goes under lots of names. Spans the globe. Got some outfits in Eastern Europe, even."

"Iron Curtain?"

"Uh-huh. And that's unusual. Ships goods to Communist China, too."

"Very enterprising."

"Yep. Britain, France, East and West Germany, Argentina, Lybia. You name it, old World-Wide's got a foot in the door. Call themselves Tell-Tex, Eurasia Comp, Intra-Flex, even something called Daisy Ltd."

"Cute."

"You bet. But it's all World-wide. Makes McCoy look like small potatoes, really penny-ante stuff."

"So why, Ross, did Hastings even *bother* with McCoy?"

"That one's easy. McCoy was a kind of front."

"Kind of?"

"Uh-huh. Because McCoy engaged in some hanky-panky of its own. Under the aegis of old Hastings. At least that's what I figure. Don't have all the hard facts. But the real business at hand went on at World-Wide. That's my guess, anyway."

"And what was this business?"

"Don't know yet."

"But you will?"

"I'd better."

"You divined all this from your stack of papers?"

"Uh-huh."

"So how?"

"Pavel. The late Professor Pavel. The guy was a whiz at languages. Vice-President in Charge of European Contracts at McCoy. Some of World-Wide's doings spilled over into McCoy. Pavel started snooping around. Began photocopying files and documents on the sly. Asked plenty of questions too. I'd bet. Hastings finally got wise, had him bumped off. But not before the damage was done."

"You sure, Ross, or just guessing again?"

Block shrugged, spread marmalade on a third piece of toast. "Who's sure of anything? Listen. Up until two years ago McCoy was the holding company that had control of World-Wide. Pavel has the papers to prove it. Then an outfit called Quintex took over. Pavel couldn't run them down. But odds have it Quintex is Hastings, just digging in deeper."

Nora sat back in her chair, looked at Block questioningly. "Just one thing in all this I don't get."

"Just one? You're doing better than I am."

"What's World-Wide guilty of?"

"*That's* what you want to know?"

Nora nodded.

"Search me," Block said.

"I wonder about you sometimes, sweetie," Nora said.

"Look," he said, "they've got to be guilty of *something*, right? Hastings bumped off Nash, and Pavel and his daughter, and took a crack at me too—"

"You can't prove that."

"I could if I had to, honey. Now Hastings has powdered out, rather tan face a grilling. Tossed McCoy aside like a used matchbook. We know World-Wide is his baby. Dig into that outfit, two to one, we come up with Charles Hastings, and what he's up to."

"Dig? Like with a shovel?"

"World-Wide's just a name in New York. No office, according to Pavel. That was a couple of years ago, so maybe it's time for another look. But Intra-Flex and Daisy Ltd., believe it or not, have Manhattan offices. Or at least they did when Pavel was on the job."

"And you're going to check them out?"

"Me, maybe. About a hundred other guys, definitely. All I've got to do is convince Felix Ashley."

"That terrible old man who owns the *Register*?"

"That's the one."

"All?"

"Don't rub it in."

CHAPTER

18

The northside Hub Credit Mart blew at 11:05 a.m.

I was a couple of miles away in an alley. I felt the ground rumble under my feet.

Sirens started to wail. Bells clanged. The police and firefighters were on the move.

I looked at my watch. "Thirteen minutes to go," I said.

Rava said, "You like to waste time, don't you?"

"No sense rushing things," I said.

"Why not?"

"Gives the opposition a chance to get interested in what they're doing."

"Always thinking of the other fellow."

"To a fault," I admitted.

At 11:18 the Ludies hit the granite Government Building. They shot up a lot of the offices, burned some Power files, barricaded the front and back doors, and left through one of the tunnels which connected the Power complex.

On their way out they stripped off their combat uniforms. Underneath, they wore business suits.

No one would've known they were Ludies if they

hadn't left leaflets and posters behind advertising the fact.

A Ludie attack on the Government Building brought out the ordinary police—those that weren't tied up at the Credit Mart—and the Secret Police and the military.

My communo beeped.

"Yeah?"

Casparian's voice came through the speaker. "Fully one-eighth of the Hub's fighting force is here."

"That's nice."

"I shall be leaving shortly."

"That's even nicer."

Casparian was holed up in a top-floor office in the Tower Building, which offered a pretty good view of the Government Complex.

"Any second now," I told Rava.

A series of satisfying explosions sounded. Rava and I exchanged glances.

"I counted six," she said.

"Yeah. Wait a second."

A seventh explosion broke the silence.

"See?"

She nodded. "How come I still feel this is crazy?"

"Because you're a pessimist."

Seven more Power strongholds—including the Tax Bureau—had been given the business.

The charges had been planted where they'd do the least harm and make the most racket.

More sirens began to moan, as if in despair at the damage which had been done. Bells clanged like a hundred church belfries gone wild.

Overhead a flock of copters buzzed by like birds of prey. They broke into two formations, one heading west, the other south.

The crafts were unmanned, directed by remote control. They were ours.

"Very impressive," Rava said.

"Yeah," I admitted. "I did it, and I'm impressed myself."

The Z-bombs began to fall from the copters on the Secret Police building, and minutes later on the army base.

Z-bombs made plenty of noise, gave off enough smoke to bury a small town. But the only way to get killed by a z-bomb was to have the casing fall on your head.

Army copters and jet balls began to pepper the sky, take after the decoys. That left the ground for us.

"The audio network should be next," I said.

"Have you no concern for the citizens?" Rava asked.

"Sure. That's what all this is about."

We waited.

Another explosion—quite close—made the ground dance.

"Well," I said, "so much for the warm-up."

"What happens now?"

"The real work begins."

The Balk electric lab was one of eight sites being hit.

Along with five credit marts.

The marts were for the syndicate.

The eight sites housed equipment I needed for the transmitter. And lots of extras the mob could carry off for itself. Fair was fair.

Rava and I were in the alley in back of the Balk lab. My communo beeped.

"Yeah?"

"We're on the second level," a voice said. "Place is full of security guards."

"Keeping them busy?"

"Busy enough."

I turned to Rava. "Okay," I said. "We're on."

*   *   *

I blasted the rear window. Wire mesh and glass splintered into little pieces.

We let the smoke clear and climbed through the hole.

We were in back of the building. Up front, by the sound of it, combat was going full tilt. Up front was where I liked it.

We took the back stairs to the second level. A metal door barred our way into the lab. A mere blaster wouldn't do here.

I removed three sticks of dynamite from my combat pouch.

We hid on the staircase as the door went blooey. Most of the wall went with it.

Rava and I helped each other over the wreckage.

I glanced around to get my bearings.

A lab attendant stepped through a door, took a gander at what had come through the wall, turned tail, and ran away.

"Smart cookie," I said.

Rava said, "He'll bring help."

I used the communo.

"Guy in a blue smock heading your way. Stop him."

"We've got our own problems," a voice told me.

The redhead and I trotted down a pale blue corridor.

Two troopers appeared at the end of the hall.

The girl and I ducked into a side corridor.

I set flame to another dynamite stick, tossed it toward the main hallways.

Rava and I ran away from there.

The hall behind us exploded. Floor, ceiling, and walls merged, became one. Rava and I picked ourselves off the floor, kept going.

No one without a pickax and shovel would manage to get through the obstacle we'd created.

We turned some more corners, came to a dead end.

I used the autohypno key; a makeshift mental floor plan of the lab sprang up in my mind.

"Through there," I said.

"Through *where*?"

"The wall."

We hid down the corridor as the fuse of another dynamite stick grew shorter.

The battle in other parts of the building—during the short-lived silence—came through loud and clear. It seemed to be inching up on us, growing closer.

The wall went up in a wave of sound. Before the wreckage had half settled, Rava and I were scuttling over the wall's remains.

The lab I wanted lay beyond.

We made our way over floorboards that shifted under our feet, dodged falling chunks of wall, side-stepped overturned tables, chairs, workbenches.

The item responsible for all this havoc was in a shattered glass case: an innocent-looking three-foot metal rod with lots of fancy wire coils on its outside and hundreds of printed circuits inside. Like almost everything else I was trying to round up, this dingus would need a bit of tinkering before I could use it. I didn't mind. It was part of my ticket out of here. And out was where I wanted to go.

My foot kicked in the glass. My hand removed the rod. I chucked it into a plastic bag.

The girl and I turned, headed back the way we'd come.

A side door burst open.

Through it poured men in uniform. Shouts, screams, gunfire came with them.

Behind them other men in street clothes darted forward. The guns in their hands boomed, crackled, and burped.

The girl and I hit the floor, rolled under a workbench.

Someone pitched a round object over our heads. It hit the wall beyond us. The wall burst into flame.

Rava and I exchanged glances; they weren't filled with joy.

I snapped on the communo.

"What's going on?" I demanded.

"Soldiers at our heels," a voice told me.

"Well, you've just chased the guards into our hiding place."

"Can't be helped. The troops are chasing *us*."

Smoke was beginning to fill the lab. So far no one had seen us. But that situation wouldn't last for long.

I looked at the crumpled wall we'd come through. Too far to reach. I looked at the pitched battle to our right. It was slowly inching toward us. The flames to our left had begun creeping along the floor.

I still had a couple of sticks of dynamite.

I used them.

I set fire to one, tossed it at the far side of the burning wall.

The girl and I crawled behind a metal case.

The wall exploded, the floor jumped, and I pitched my last stick down between us and the battlers.

The floor went up with a roar. Rava and I were halfway to the now crumbled wall. Tables, cabinets, chairs danced as if acquiring a will of their own.

Smoke was everywhere.

Rava and I crouched under a workbench.

I spoke into the communo. "We're moving out. Cover us."

A barrage of gunfire behind us sent splinters flying in all directions.

That was all the answer we needed.

Using what was left of the lab furnishings for cover, we crawled toward the wall.

Smoke, flame, wreckage, and a lot of men busy killing each other gave us all the cover we needed.

We climbed through a hole in the wall, crawled along the corridor, got to our feet, and ran for it.

The staircase took us down. No one was waiting for us on ground level. We stepped over the pile of bricks, which led into the alley.

Daylight was fading. We were in between two brick walls. We could see none of the festivities taking place outside. But we could hear them all right. It sounded as if a small-scale war was in progress.

"What have you done?" Rava asked.

"Something bad by the sound of it," I said.

We used the back streets to take us out of the war zone. We weren't the only ones there. People were running for all they were worth. We ran with them.

The bubbletop careened along the mountain road. Five others followed at our heels. A large truck followed that. The mob was making its getaway with the spoils. The mob, in this case, was me.

Darkness seemed to squeeze down on our mini-caravan. The mountains rose around us like endless black walls crowding us in. A solid sheet of clouds blotted out the sky.

One lone cyclist raced before us—our guide. Only his head and tail lights lit our way. These vanished every time he hit a curve. Radar beams attached to each vehicle saved us from riding into a mountain or each other.

What the trip lacked in safety it made up in excitement. Too bad I'd had enough excitement to last me a couple of decades.

Casparian drove. Rava and I sat squeezed in beside him.

Casparian said, "We seem to have most of the items you sought."

"Most?"

The fat man shrugged a shoulder. "Our emissaries of the underworld did their level best."

"What happened?"

"Some of the articles you requested were simply not available."

"Come on," I said.

"We looked for them in the wrong places, perhaps."

"Great intelligence setup you boys've got."

"Or," Casparian said, "they could not be safely removed. Or they were removed but retaken by the Power."

"How much equipment are we talking about?"

"Eight or nine pieces."

"Know what they are?"

"Not yet. We will take inventory once we reach the laboratory. But I would not be concerned, Siscoe, if I were you."

"You're not me," I pointed out.

Casparian smiled. "There is still ample time to procure them. You will be gone for a good week. And by the time you have returned—provided you do, of course—the remainder of the items will be waiting for you."

"A week, huh?"

"That is an optimistic assessment. The rulers of North Xcroth are even more dictatorial than the Power. The Q product is a closely guarded secret. It may very well be unobtainable."

"I'll take that chance. You got my itinerary worked out?"

"To the last detail. Up to the border, that is. From there on, Siscoe, you are on your own."

I slept late the next morning. I was in no mood to get rolling. Yesterday's fireworks had taken their toll. The fracas in town had been one war too many. I felt old and decrepit, as though my sinews and muscles had begun to unravel.

I lay in a wide bed on the second floor of the Fellowship's mountain hideaway and wondered what my pal Block was up to. By now he should've polished off whatever Earth troubles there were and be back on the Control World. He'd noticed my absence, but what could he do about it? No rescue mission could be mounted, no last-minute intervention planned. I was so far off the beaten track that a dozen Blocks in a hundred lifetimes wouldn't find me. I wasn't even so sure he'd bother looking very hard. The fact that we shared the Chairman's mind didn't exactly make us blood brothers.

This last thought got me out of bed. A shave and shower had me feeling almost normal. I went down to breakfast.

Four of us sat around the long table eating. I wasn't the only one who'd slept late.

"Didn't expect to see you here," I said to Targ between mouthfuls of some local grain that tasted vaguely like chicken. I was starting to miss chicken.

"City's under martial law," he said. "A good time to go on vacation. It was all I could do to slip through their net."

"Bet the Power's stewing," I said.

"I can assure you, Siscoe, that it is far worse than that," Worts said. "Mass arrests. Wholesale detentions. Large parts of the Hub roped off. Oh, yes, it is definitely an excellent time to be elsewhere."

Rava said, "Aren't you ashamed, Siscoe, for all the trouble you've caused? The damage? The innocent people arrested?"

"No one's innocent," I told her. "Besides, the only way you'll get the Power off your backs is if I get out of here and back to the Control World."

"And what happens then?" Casparian asked.

"The Galactic Arm comes in here and mops up."

"It will be that easy?" Casparian said.

"Sure. The Power's got a lot going for it, pal. But it can't hold a candle to the Arm. Your boys are strictly minor-league by comparison."

"So we substitute one despotism for another?" Casparian said.

"Let's not panic," I told him. "You've got an ace."

Targ smiled. "*You*, of course."

"Yeah, me. The big boss himself, the guy who runs the Galactic Arm. You've got my word for it."

Rava said, "What's that worth?"

"Plenty. Look at the alternative."

"He's right," Targ said. "There is no alternative."

"I am aware of that," Casparian said.

"Then why sweat it?" I asked.

Casparian shrugged. "Many have begun with the best intentions and been corrupted by the power they wield."

"Not this baby." I grinned at him. "I won't be around long enough for that. Just long enough to set up a smooth Galactic operation, one you'll like, pal; then I move on."

"Some leader," Rava said.

"I'm not," I told her. "Lucky you."

"The Brotherhood," Casparian said, "should by no means be confused with the Fellowship."

"Wouldn't dream of it," I told him. "Anyway, I'm not applying for membership. Just asking for help."

"That is my point. The Brotherhood is far smaller; it is, you might say, devoted solely to crime. You will find none of the affiliates which we possess: industry, the military, the Secret Police. It will make your mission that much harder."

"Perhaps impossible," Targ said.

I grinned at him. "I'll let you know."

Dusk was slipping over the mountains. Long shadows were visible through the lab windows. The terrain didn't look any too inviting. I sighed.

Worts said, "I must object again."

"Can it, Worts," I said.

"My presence is uncalled-for," Worts said. "Believe me, I will only be a hindrance."

"You're our best bet for getting in and out in one piece," I told him. "You go."

"We are all committing suicide," Worts cried.

"Pull yourself together," Targ said.

"That is simple for *you* to say," Worts said. "You are not going to a certain death."

"No one is going to his death," I said with more optimism than I felt.

"If you know so much," Worts said, "why do you need us?"

"Your compensation, Worts, will be ample," Casparian said.

"A corpse has no need of credit," Worts said.

"The issue is closed," Casparian said.

Worts shrugged.

I said, "How is Jilks taking all this?"

"If, by 'all this,' you mean your departure," Casparian said, "he is unaware of it. If you mean the upheaval in town, he is no doubt somewhat peeved. The bounty taken in, while considerable, in no way compensates for the massive reprisals taking place. The syndicate will be severely shaken."

"I called him before leaving," Targ said. "Despite the curfew, he was gone. Hiding out, I'd imagine."

It was dark outside now.

"It's time," I said.

"I wish you the best of luck," Casparian said. "The

transmitter will be all but assembled upon your return. I shall supervise myself."

"And I'll supervise him," Targ said.

Rava came through the door.

"Bubble's packed. We're late."

I got up from my seat. "Come on, Worts."

"This is madness," Worts said.

"Yeah, along with a lot of other things."

We drove most of the night, heading northeast, away from the Hub. We skirted the gray towns where the noncitizens sweated at their old-style assembly lines. We saw distant lights from factory windows and the glow of flames reaching through giant chimneys, smelled smoke rolling over the countryside. The plants were as out of date as last year's calendar; the Power was in the next century as far as tech went, but they were sitting on their finds. The setup had more than a couple of screws loose.

Flatlands gave way to foothills. We shot past the midtowns, dwelling places of class C citizens. They were dark, silent hamlets, as if someone had locked each resident away and shorted the lights.

The highways were almost deserted. Internal passports were hard to come by; the populace stayed put.

We hit two checkpoints, roadblocks which tagged us with spotter eyes before we could turn tail and run.

Targ had come up with a batch of papers that made us out to be top Hub moguls on a business jaunt. No one wanted to mess with business. We got the Xcroth version of the red-carpet treatment and were waved through.

When two of the Xcroth suns began to peek over the horizon, we checked into a local travelers' haven and caught forty winks.

Nighttime found us out on the road again. We kept

to the back lanes. Even with our class A IDs the less attention we attracted the better. No way to tell if anyone had spilled the beans about us in the Hub, or some raid turned up evidence of our jaunt. Our best bet was to keep low. We kept.

The mountains got taller, the forest longer. Highways became meandering dirt roads. When daylight came again, we were high up on the side of a mountain. Checkpoints and stray traffic had long been left behind. We had the mountains to ourselves. We didn't stop now, but pushed on, the three of us taking turns at the control stick. After a while we reached the jungle.

The road came to an end. We left our bubbletop under a large tree and took off on foot. Rava acted as guide. Three suns—two mere dots in the sky—shone overhead. Worts began to complain and didn't stop till we hit the smugglers' shack.

The shack was a makeshift affair of tin and tar. No one lived there; it was only a contact point. The nameless old guy who showed up a couple of hours later took us through thick foliage. Birds chirped, screeched, and hooted. Things scurried in the underbrush. The four of us trudged along.

One of the suns had vanished by the time we sighted the clearing. Three men, also nameless, led us through more thicket. I lost track of time, of direction. I was beginning to think wistfully of the travelers' haven when our guides pulled up. The tall one pointed to a break in the trees.

"There's a road through there," he said. "Follow it."

"And we hit North Xcroth?" I said.

"This *is* North Xcroth," he said.

"We pay them?" I asked the girl.

"It's been taken care of," she said.

Our guides faded into the woods without another word.

The path was easy to find. It wound its way through thinning trees and shrubbery.

We came out on a level plane. Ankle-high yellow plants stretched toward the horizon. Bluish hills were visible in the distance. More trees were over on the left.

"Where the hell are we?" I said.

"In the wilderness," Worts said, "where we shall surely perish. A man my age should not be called upon to make such a perilous journey. The stress alone is enough to do damage. It is madness."

"You done?" Rava asked.

The little man wiped his forehead with a hanky. "I believe so."

"I've made this trip before," Rava said. "I've been liaison to the Brotherhood. That's why I was chosen to come with you. We go that way, through the trees. It's not very far."

"North Xcroth is a terrible place," Worts said.

"Come on," I told him.

He came.

The cabin was made of logs. It was empty except for one cot. The girl stretched out and went to sleep. Worts and I stayed outdoors. He paced. I sat against a wall and dozed. About an hour crawled by. Insects buzzed around us, and something yapped in the woods. The three suns were back in the sky. Only a few pinkish clouds kept them company. I was all set to call it a day and go hunting for a tennis court and swimming pool when the man showed up. He came strolling out of the woods, a medium-size guy in need of a shave.

"Just the pair of you, eh?" he said.

"One more inside," I said.

"Okay. Leave anything that ties you to the other side here. I got a brace of new IDs for you. You're now class A citizens of Ludie Province. That's the capital, see?"

"You mean we are Ludies," Worts said.

"Yeah, Ludies."

"I'd rather die," Worts said.

"That's real easy to arrange. Lotsa folks who ain't never set foot in the South, and wouldn't want to, get shot for Hubbies every day."

"Hubbies, huh?" I said.

"That's you, brother," the guy said.

"It is intolerable," Worts said.

I said, "I've been called worse."

"Snap it up," the guy said. "We ain't got all day."

I went in and woke Rava.

We buried our Hub papers under a floorboard and set out through the woods.

A bubbletop was waiting for us on a gravel road.

We piled in and drove away from there.

There was probably a big difference between North and South that any native of Xcroth could've picked out with his eyes closed. To me both sides looked alike. We rode through drab townlets where ours seemed to be the only vehicle on the road. The few inhabitants out on the street stared at us dully.

We rolled through factory towns that looked like replicas of earth in the 1920s. We scooted by an army barracks which seemed to belong to another century, one far in the future. We hit a slum town that was mostly made up of tin and wood shacks. This Xcroth was some world.

Ludie took us half the day to get to. My legs were cramped from too much sitting, my eyes bleary from gazing out the window. Conversation had died hours ago.

Slowly, buildings began to rise around us, to grow in height and widen. More bubbletops were on the road now. No trees were in sight; man-made structures had taken their place.

The buildings kept getting taller. Soon they were standing shoulder to shoulder, stretching in all directions, one massive complex that let through mere slits of sky which now seemed more gray than pink. There was plenty of noise, too, crowded streets, and transparent tunnel tubes that whisked passengers on their way.

I yawned, noticed I was hungry again, and casually turned my head to look out the opposite side window.

There was a square, surrounded by tall, imposing structures—the Government Complex. In the square's center was a large statue up on a marble pedestal. It was looking my way. I looked back and nearly fell off my seat.

My old pal Ganz the telepath was cast in plastodeck, riding motionlessly and forever on his plastodeck steed. He looked right at home, too.

CHAPTER

19

Felix Ashley, a dignified sixty-nine with a full head of snow-white hair, white mustache, cleft chin, glasses, and blue pin-striped suit, glared at Block and Ben Cohen from behind his wide desk on the top floor of the *Register* building and said one word: "Poppycock!"

Ben Cohen, shifting uneasily in his chair, said, "If it pans out, Mr. Ashley, it'll be one hell of a story."

"*If*," Ashley said. "If. If."

Block said, "I can't prove a whole lot now—"

"You can't prove *anything*," Ashley snapped.

"But," Block continued, "I think I can make a pretty good stab at it." He patted his briefcase. "Based on the documents I've acquired."

Ashley snorted. "Bah!"

"Mr. Ashley," Cohen said, "I've seen what Block's got; it's worth thinking about."

"So you say," Ashley said. "But look who is offering us this bonanza. A man who has seen fit to walk away from his job for the better part of a year, and comes up with a cock-and-bull explanation that even a child would find hard to swallow."

"Mr. Ashley," Cohen said, "Block *was* on the Bowery, was a guest at the Men's Shelter."

"The police can verify that much," Block said.

Ashley shook his finger at Block. "Your drinking problems are no concern of mine, Block. What happened to your Marty Nash exposé? You had five valuable reporters wasting their time, and my money, on that piece of nonsense. And now you want an even greater expenditure of men and resources. For *what*?"

Block said, "The book's not closed on this Nash business, Mr. Ashley."

"It is as far as I'm concerned," Ashley said.

Cohen said, "I understand, Mr. Ashley, the project does look kind of fishy. But you're wrong."

"*Wrong*?" Ashley said. "*Wrong*?"

"There's too much at stake here to just walk away," Cohen said. "The thing's too big. If we don't move on it someone else will."

"I can't sit on it," Block said. "My first loyalty's to this paper. But if you turn me down flat, Mr. Ashley, I'll have to go elsewhere."

Ashley said, "Is that a threat?"

"Uh-uh. Just a statement."

"Block doesn't mean take this to the competition," Cohen said.

"What *does* he mean?"

"The cops, maybe; the feds," Cohen said.

"Listen," Block said. "Anyone I give this to, sooner or later, the story gets out. No way to stop it. By dropping it in your lap, Mr. Ashley, I'm taking a chance."

"*Chance*?" Ashley's face turned beet red. "*You're* taking a chance?"

"There've been some killings already. There could be more; reporters aren't equipped to handle that."

Cohen said, "He's got a point, Mr. Ashley."

"Listen. We've got to move in, move out. Get our evidence before Hasting stumbles. He finds out what we're up to, it'll just drive him deeper underground. That's the other chance. Blowing the whole game by having amateurs snooping around."

Ashley said, "Are you calling my reporters, your colleagues, *amateurs*, Block?"

Block shrugged. "That's what they are, at least in this. But if they move fast, maybe they can pull it off. We're dealing with an intricate, highly complex organization—World-Wide, going under a variety of names. There'll be a lot of intracompany transactions, though, and that'll give us our wedge, let us get a foot in the door."

"Could make history," Cohen said.

"Shouldn't cost that much," Block said.

"Sure, it's a gamble, Mr. Ashley," Cohen said. "But this paper's grown fat on gambles. From what I've seen of Block's documentation, it's a gamble I've got to take."

Ashley glowered at them. "One week. That's all you get. One week. And if this doesn't work out, you're both fired!"

"Jesus H. Christopher," Ben Cohen said.

"Lemme buy you a drink, Ben."

"Buy me a bottle, for Chrissakes. Make that two."

"This'll pan out, Ben, don't worry."

"Don't worry, he says."

"You'll see," Block said.

They walked up the corridor to Cohen's office, the editor mopping his brow.

"I'll see, eh? What I'll see is an early retirement. Like next week, maybe. And me in the prime of life."

They turned into Cohen's office. Cohen sank into his desk chair, sighed, reached inside a bottom drawer, came up with a bottle of bourbon, and two pony glasses, and poured each of them a shot. "To crime," he said.

Both men drank. Block moved his chair closer to the editor's desk, said, "That guy Ashley's a tough old goat, isn't he?"

"Yeah. And he didn't get where he is by buying pipedreams. This clinches it, I must be off my rocker, no two ways about it."

"Now, Ben."

"Don't now Ben me, son. I know when I've gone around the bend, lost a couple marbles. I wouldn't bet more than two cents out of a buck that there's anything but a lot of eyewash in this dumb yarn of yours. And here I go laying my job on the line, backing it. Can you beat that? Forty years in the business and it all goes down the drain because in a moment of mental derangement, I swallow this dimwit tale of yours."

"We'll make history together, Ben."

"We'll end up on relief."

"Whatever we do," Block said, "we'd better do it quick."

"Yeah, quick. So what's the pitch?"

"How's the European staff these days?"

"Just like it was a year ago."

"None, eh?"

"None."

"That figures. Stringers?"

"We've still got 'em."

"Any good?"

"A couple."

"Hire some extras?"

"It'll cost."

"Not our money."

"Yeah. Thank God for something."

"Gotta have the best on this."

"The best. Know something? You're nuts, Block."

"Sure. Anyone in China?"

"China?"

"World-Wide's got an in there."

"Christ."

"Japan, too."

"Have a heart, Block."

"Too expensive?"

"Break the kitty."

"Ashley's good for it."

"He'll kill us."

"Ben, we can't tiptoe around on this. We have to go for broke."

"Broke."

"Uh-huh. Anyone in Argentina?"

"Yeah."

"Okay."

Block opened his briefcase, removed a neatly typed sheet of paper, handed it to Cohen. The editor glared at it.

"You got thirty, forty names here."

"Uh-huh."

"All different."

"All World-Wide."

"You sure?"

Block shrugged.

"Christ."

"That, Ben, is what we have to find out. Who they are, what they buy, sell, manufacture."

"Simple stuff, eh?"

"Yep. Last five are U.S. firms."

"Ross."

"Yes, Ben."

"You're asking a lot."

"I know."

"This don't work, we really will be fired."

"I know."

"But I'm gonna do it."

"Thanks, Ben."

"Know why?"

"Sure. You're in too deep to pull out."

"Yeah. That's why."

"Me too, Ben."

Nighttime:

The truck came out of nowhere. One moment the street was empty, the next, a huge two-tonner was roaring down on him.

Block jerked his wheel sharply to the right; the car lurched onto the sidewalk.

Sparks lit the darkness as the two vehicles scraped fenders.

Block's auto seemed to rise into the air, tilt sideways, right itself with a teeth-rattling crunch.

The truck, headlights off, driverless, hurtled by.

Block used his brakes; the car skidded to a halt. He twisted around to stare wide-eyed behind him.

The truck slammed into a lamp post.

An instant of silence, then the truck exploded. A huge sheet of flame reached into the darkness.

The night seemed to shake—along with Block.

"Jesus," Block said.

Lights were snapping on behind closed windows. People would be out on the street any second.

Block's trembling hands worked frantically to get the engine started again. It was as if shock had robbed him of his ability to use his fingers.

The engine caught; the car, whining as though in pain, rattled forward.

"Jesus," Block said again.

He took the car back onto the street.

People had come out of their houses, were gaping at the flaming truck. No one noticed Block.

Carefully he drove away from the wreck.

His hands were damp, his clothes stuck to his body like Scotch tape.

A small smile twitched at left corner of his mouth. *Pabst had gotten his message.*

CHAPTER
20

Rafe said, "This Ganz guy is a kinda legend, see? He showed up here maybe ten years ago. Anyway, that's the word I got. The whole thing at the time was like, you know, under wraps. Only the big boys knew, the Big Three who run the show here, the Governing Committee. You get that?"

I told him I got it.

He poured me another drink. Rava and Worts were still nursing theirs. This Rafe was a short, compact, thick-featured guy who was high up in the Brotherhood. He was our contact. When Casparian had warned me that the Brotherhood was just a pale shadow of the Fellowship, he had known what he was talking about. The three of us hadn't been taken to a towering skyscraper in the ritziest section of town, but to a small, dingy three-story brick house on the far side of Ludie. The three of us and Rafe, our host, were camped in the basement. There was a lamp, a table, four chairs, four glasses, and a bottle of joy juice. The floor was concrete, the walls damp brick. A trickle of water wound its way down one wall, made a puddle on the floor. I'd come a long way to be here. I could picture a couple thousand better places without working up a sweat. Anyone could.

Rafe went on, "Okay, but I got ways of finding out things, see? And this guy Ganz, I find out, he's maybe an offworlder. And he's teamed up with the Big Three. Anyway, someone tries to pull off a coup just then. That ain't nothin' new. We useta have lotsa 'em here. But no more. This coup, it never gets off the ground. The chumps who signed up for the push get smeared all over the landscape. The word is, this Ganz brings with him like all kindsa superweapons. No one on Xcroth ever seen anything like it. Know what I mean?"

I told him I knew.

"Okay. Them three guys, the Big Three, they're still in charge. See, they got these weapons; they like put together this spy system. You can't beat it. They know what's goin' on, got the inside track on what the opposition's up to. Them guys is fixed for life. This Ganz, he put 'em over for keeps. You figure maybe things get better here in the North? Forget it. Things, they gets worse. Nothin' this guy Ganz brings gets down to the citizens. You get me?"

"Yeah, I got you."

"Okay. The Big Three, the army, the spy squads, they got all this stuff padlocked, are sittin' on it. This Ganz meanwhile does a fade. Maybe he's dead, right? Maybe he's gone back where he's come from. Maybe he's holed-up somewhere. Maybe the Big Three knows, maybe they don't. No one knows, that's for sure. Anyway, they puts this statue up in the square. And this Ganz makes the history books. He's the guy squelched the coup, made the North a stronghold, see? He's given the credit. The books call him a man of the people, a guy who rose through the ranks, helped when it counted most. Then retired or somethin'. That's a lotta crap. He's s a stinkin' offworlder, and whatever he was up to, you gotta bet it was somethin' rotten, see? That's the dirt on this Ganz guy; that's all there is."

I said, "It couldn't've been ten years ago. Ganz was light-years away from the Control World, just working his way up the ladder on his own world. He couldn't've gotten here."

"Yeah, sure, if that's the way you want it," Rafe said. "Only it *was* ten years ago. Now what's this about you wanting this fuel pile, this Q thing, huh?"

It took a day to size up the situation, get the lay of the land.

Worts expended some of his limited mind power, tuned in on the opposition.

Rafe sent his boys snooping.

Rava and I took a tour of Ludie.

Like it's southern counterpart, the city was a study in contrasts: sleek towers, rotting slums, long stretches of drab box-houses, home of the class B segment. There were plenty of those.

A lot of guys in jet-black uniforms seemed to be all over the place. They rode by in bubbletops, paraded the streets in twos and threes. They carried a small arsenal with them. Twice, we were stopped by patrols, frisked, had our IDs checked. We passed with flying colors. A couple of citizens next to us weren't so lucky, were hauled off in the Ludie version of the paddy wagon. No one gave them a second glance.

Rava and I went on our way. We didn't exactly sprint around the corner, but we didn't dawdle either.

I said, "How's this stack up against the South?"

"Almost the same."

"It doesn't look the same."

The redhead smiled. "You weren't there on a bad day."

* * *

Rafe said, "Could be worse. This thing you want, this fuel, they're still foolin' with it in the Projects Complex."

"That's what?" I said.

"State lab. They come up with new poison gases, disintegrators, blasters, stuff like that. This must be somethin' along them lines, right? And that's a break, see? If it were on an army base, we'd be up the creek. This way we got a crack at it."

Worts nodded. "I have scrutinized them. There are possibilities. Changes of the guard, as it were, that we could utilize to our advantage. But I must tell you, there is frightful danger. My own talents are depleted, but still adequate. I shall probe again, carefully, of course."

"Sure," I said.

"One thing I can assure you."

"Yeah?"

"I shall not go within links of this operation once it is in progress. I shall assist you from afar. In any case, I will need all my energy to cope with our foes. I shall not communicate with you psychically, Siscoe, but through mechanical means. This entire operation could end in catastrophe. I am no fool."

"You're a damn hero, Worts."

"And I could dispense with your sarcasm too. After all, what are you without me?"

"Lost."

"Quite right."

We made our play on the third day.

Twenty men in black jumpsuits and armed to the teeth moved silently to their posts around the Projects Complex. The buildings were inside surrounded by a wire fence. We were outside.

Rafe had turned up a fine bunch of cutthroats. There was Lutz the safecracker, and Anst the strongarm specialist. Lapky could pick locks. Greld knew how to play havoc with alarm systems. Quins had once been a lab tech before the joy juice got to him. He'd spent a couple of years in the complex. Rack blew up doors and other objects that might get in the way. The rest of our crew were assault troops. Ordinarily, I wouldn't have wanted to meet any of them on a dark street; right now they were a godsend.

Dark night shrouded our presence. The air was still.

Our expert—Greld—went to work on the alarm wires. He had them shorted in an eyeblink.

Laser beams cut through the wire fence, made holes large enough for men to crawl through.

We waited for our cue, shivering in the breeze.

Rava's voice sounded through my communo-ear-plug: "They're changing the guard."

"Thanks," I said into my collar communo. I tapped another digit. "Let's move," I said to Anst.

I waved my party of three through the hole in the wall, then followed at their heels.

We used no light. Infra-goggles showed us the way.

We sprinted across a courtyard, passed two dark-ened structures, ran under a large arch and up five wide stone steps to the lab.

Greld dropped to his hands and knees, crawled forward. Reaching into his tool pouch, he came up with a slim electro-scrambler; suction cups pinned it to the wall. The spotter eye overhead went blind.

Lapky got the door open in less than thirty seconds.

The rest of our crew came running, dark shadows against the darker night. Four of them wore the gray uniforms of the Complex. Silently they slipped through the doorway.

A gray-uniformed Quins led the way.

The rest spread out, went off on their respective rounds.

I and a trio of cohorts trailed after Quins.

We entered a domed hall. The floor was marble, the ceiling high above us.

A voice in my ear said, "Stop."

I put a hand on Quins's shoulder.

Rava's voice sounded in my ear again. "Two guards in corridor nine. They're walking your way."

"What about the other pair?" I whispered.

"Anst and Kard have taken their place."

We flattened ourselves against the marble walls. Statues were never stiller.

Two pairs of footsteps sounded from corridor nine, grew louder.

Other footsteps reached us. These came from corridor four, which ran perpendicular to the hall we were in.

Presently two distant figures appeared. They were clad in guard gray. Slowly they moved toward the center of the hall.

Two other figures emerged from corridor four. They also wore guard uniforms.

One of the guards from nine dropped behind the other. The stunner in his hand was blocked from sight until he used it. No sound. The pair of victims merely stiffened, tumbled forward. They lay on the floor like two store dummies.

Anst and his buddy joined us.

"How many did you chew up?"

Anst grinned, "Eight. Stripped the first two. Caught the rest napping."

I spoke into my communo: "How's it going upstairs?"

"They heard nothing," Rava's voice said into my ear. "Wait till I give you the go-ahead. The guards are still too close to the staircase."

"Righto," I said. "Our boys in place?"

"All of them."

I let out my breath. "Okay." To my men I said, "Stand by."

We stood.

"Move," the girl said.

We moved.

A wide marble staircase led up to the second level. We lurked there, jumped the guards on their return trip. There were more of us than them. The fracas didn't last long.

We left our victims stretched out on the floor, moved on.

All through the Complex our boys—guided by Worts via Rava—went into action. By the time we reached lab seven, most of the guards were in slumberland, and the rest were being mopped up one by one.

We pulled up in front of a pair of giant doors. They were made of solid metal.

Rack squatted in front of the barrier.

"How's it look?" I asked.

"A cinch," Rack said.

"Okay," I said. "Shoot the works."

The rest of us hid in a side corridor as Rack did his stuff.

He joined us. A second later the floor jumped under our feet and the walls seemed to do a shimmy.

When the smoke cleared the doors were no more than twisted hunks of metal.

No alarms deafened our ears; no guards popped up with blazing guns. The whole shebang had been neutralized.

We marched through the wreckage.

Three white, shiny corridors faced us.

"This way," Quins said.

We followed Quins down the middle hallway, passed open doorways, labs filled with glass, metal, and plastic hardware. We didn't bother taking stock. We followed Quins.

We went through a doorless doorway into a wide, high-ceilinged room.

A giant floor safe filled the center of the lab.

"In there," Quins said.

I turned to Lutz. "Think you can handle that?"

Lutz shrugged. "Let's see."

He strolled over to the safe, dropped to one knee.

"That will not be necessary," a booming voice said.

A large viewscreen lit up on the far wall. From it, the face of Jilks beamed down at me and my crew of culprits. He grinned. "I've been expecting you, Siscoe."

I stared up at the giant viewscreen with its enlarged grinning face. The word "surprised" didn't describe my feelings. "Stunned witless" hardly scratched the surface. Maybe, if I got through this day alive, I'd think up the word; I had my doubts.

Jilks said, "Don't look so amazed, Siscoe. You never had a chance."

"Never, huh?" I heard myself say. I could still talk. That was something. Too bad something wasn't good enough.

"We were ahead of you every step of the way," Jilks said.

"We?"

"The Big Three."

"You're teamed up with them?"

"I *am* them."

"Knock it off, Jilks. You're nothing but a two-bit stoolie. You had it made, but that wasn't good enough for you, was it? You sold out your pals for a few lousy credits. What did the Ludies give you, Jilks? How much did it take to buy you?"

The giant head on the viewscreen shook itself; a thin smile played around its lips. "My name is Nardlow, and I am the centerpiece of the Big Three."

"Nardlow?" I said stupidly.

The giant head nodded.

"Why would Nardlow want to play at being a South Xcroth hood?" I asked reasonably enough.

"Because it is the plan."

"You've got a plan?"

"Who doesn't?"

"Very deep," I said.

The giant head nodded genially, "So it should be. It is the plan of Ganz."

"Ah-ha," I said, as though that actually explained something. The fact that I'd managed to get the words out encouraged me—only not enough.

"You know of Ganz, then?" the giant head said.

I admitted it.

"You will be of use," Nardlow told me.

I thought of a number of uses I could have for this guy, and didn't like any of them. "Ganz your boss?" I asked.

"He is the leader."

"He tip you off?"

"Our leader *in absentia*. No, it wasn't necessary for Ganz to alert us. I had your number from the very beginning, Siscoe, you and your ragtag crew. That's why we set up this viewscreen to accommodate you. I myself am many links away."

"So when Worts gave this place the once-over you wouldn't be here," I said.

The giant head smirked. "I could have taken you in the South, Siscoe."

"If you'd known where I was."

"Yes, that was an obstacle. But I was sure you would come here, in search of your Q product. And I made the necessary arrangements. There are laser weapons trained on you, Siscoe, from every side of the room. They operate by remote control. The switch is within my reach. Do we understand each other?"

"Yeah."

"Good. You know Ganz personally?"

I said I did.

"Where is he now?" Nardlow demanded.

"You don't know?"

"If I knew, would I ask you?"

"I suppose not. Your Ganz tried a power play on the Control World, and came up a loser. Last I heard, he was running for his life."

"So you don't know his whereabouts?"

"That's what I don't know."

The large head wagged at me. "Have no fear, Siscoe, Ganz will turn up. The man is indestructible."

"So he said."

Nardlow smiled. "It's been a long time since Ganz put in an appearance on Xcroth."

"Maybe that's because he was in the clink," I said.

"In prison?"

"Yeah. Along with me. Not so indestructible now, huh?"

Nardlow shrugged. "What does it matter? He got out, didn't he? Ganz will always prevail, Siscoe; it's his destiny. Just as it is mine to rule this world."

"You, huh?"

"At the telepath's behest, of course."

"Yeah, of course."

"I'm one of the selected, Siscoe; my counterparts exist throughout the galaxy, a few to each world. We all follow the master's plan. On Xcroth I am Ganz's sole disciple."

"Good for you, pal."

"You scoff. But the plan works brilliantly. For ten years I have managed to maintain the status quo here, to play North and South off against each other. My agents are everywhere. We wait for the Master's return. With him at my side, the opposition will crumble. Our world will assume it's rightful place in the galaxy, with me at its helm."

"You don't say?"

"But I do."

"Kind of spilling the beans a bit, aren't you? All this running off at the mouth could land you in the soup, pal."

"Not through your doing, Siscoe. You are doomed."

"You don't kid around, huh, Nardlow?"

"I bear you no personal grudge, but you are a menace to the plan, my friend. You are an offworlder, and you have had contact with Ganz. I could speak to you as to no other. But your fate is sealed."

"Because of this plan?"

"Of course."

"Don't be a sap, Nardlow. Your plan's old hat. Ganz is on the run. And before that he was doing time in the slammer. He's no superman; he's got his hands full just staying alive these days. You and your backwoods world are probably no more than past history to him now. Otherwise he'd've been back long ago. Think it over, Nardlow. I'm your best bet, your ticket to the universe. You don't need Ganz. Team up with me and I'll hand you this world on a silver platter, and a lot more besides."

"But you're wrong, Siscoe. Ganz foresaw a lengthy interval before his return. That too is part of the plan. Xcroth is cut off from the rest of the galaxy. A black hole in space interferes with the transmissions, has put our world out of sync. Your arrival here is simply a fluke. Ganz himself is not due for two years. He *is* a superman, my friend; never doubt that. For me to change sides now would be an act of suicidal idiocy."

Nardlow leaned forward, his eyes fixed on me. His hand reached toward something off camera. I didn't need two guesses to know what that something was.

I glanced up at the ceiling. I couldn't spot the laser muzzles, but they'd be there, all right. And by the time they'd done their work nothing would be left alive in this room.

I half turned toward the door. My crew of house-breakers had gotten the message too, were hotfooting it for the nearest exit. Only they'd never make it. And neither would I.

I looked back at the giant face. It had lost its smile. Large beads of sweat coated its forehead. The eyes were glassy, the brow wrinkled, as if it had been struck by a thought too horrible to contemplate.

The arm, I noticed, was about as mobile as a wooden Indian's.

Was Nardlow having an attack of conscience? Was the prospect of blowing away a group of people proving too much for him? I wouldn't have bet two cents on it.

Very slowly, like a tree rotted at its base, Nardlow began to topple; the giant face slid from the screen. A blank wall took its place. The sound of a body hitting the floor could be heard over the audio.

The girl's voice sounded in my ear. "Hurry."

"What happened?"

"Worts took him out."

"The whammy?"

"Yes. But you're on your own now."

"*Why*?"

"Worts is on the floor."

"Passed out?"

"Dead maybe. It was too much for him."

"Christ."

I spoke two words into the communo. "Condition red."

My buddies had halted at the door, all set to make their getaway.

I said, "This Nardlow's out cold. We've got possibly five minutes to swipe the fuel pile. And anything else that's in that safe. You guys game? Or do I gotta do all this myself?"

The sirens came alive when we were five blocks from the Complex. Worts wasn't around to run interference for us. I gunned the bubbletop, turned into a dark side street. The rest of the vehicles—loaded with miscreants—took off in different directions. It was every man for himself now. Lutz and Quins were by my side, our prize, the fuel pile, in back. Lutz gave me directions. The bubbletop twisted through the streets like a snake over hot coals.

The sirens faded, were left behind.

I turned the car toward Rafe's hideaway.

Nobody got in our way.

The girl's voice came to me across the distance and night:

"Siscoe, they've got Rafe!"

"Got him?"

"Place is crawling with police. House is blocked off. Searchlights everywhere."

I said, "Where are you?"

"Headed away from here."

"They spot you?"

"Too busy shooting up Rafe. He's got half his gang with him. It's a small war. I just turned and beat it."

"Worts with you?"

"The back seat."

"He okay?"

"He's alive, that's all."

"What street you on?"

She gave me the numbers.

I said, "Pull over, sit tight. I'll pick you up in a jiffy."

I turned to Lutz. "How do we get to Eighteen and Three-oh-seven?"

Lutz told me.
We got.

Lutz and Quins drove away in the bubbletop.
The street was dark, empty.
I pulled back on the lever; three wheels moved under me. Houses, trees, streetlamps slid by outside.
Worts lay in the back seat; he was snoring. The fuel pile, wrapped in a canvas bag, kept him company.
"Where are we going?" Rava asked.
"Home," I told her.

CHAPTER
21

Block entered his flat, got out his Control World tool kit, wired both doors and windows, put together some makeshift spotter eyes, clamped them in the hallway and on the building's front and back door.

The next day he bought some electronics supplies on Canal Street, put together a small arsenal of gadgets he'd culled from the Chairman's mind.

Then he waited.

The reports started dribbling in the next night, continued throughout the week. First from Europe—Germany, Belgium, Spain. Then Japan, South Korea, Brazil, and Argentina checked in. More Europe: France, Italy. Then a report from South Africa. It didn't matter what names the firms went under. They were all World-Wide. And whatever they dabbled in, the thing they had in common, did most of, was computers.

Cohen's stringers had hardly earned their pay. Almost no digging was required. The whole World-Wide operation—whether it was Tell-Tex, Eurasia Comp, Quintex, or some other outfit—was open and aboveboard. All the stringers had to do was nose around a bit, talk to a few people in the business, maybe even drop in at a World-Wide sales office or factory, and then cable back their reports. Nothing to it.

Block sat at his kitchen table, leafing through the papers. It was 5:15. Sunlight shone through a west window. Dusk was only a half hour away. He sighed, reached for his coffee cup. World-Wide was a sterling example of rectitude. They paid their bills, forked over their taxes to the last penny, and built computers that were solid, made to last. Only one small point rankled. Half the World-Wide outfits were selling their goods at a dead loss, had been doing so for the better part of five years. One helluva way to make a profit.

He parked his car on a side street. It was 11:20. The night was dark, empty. Solitary streetlamps lit up the cold pavements. Block raised the collar of his trench coat. A strong wind blew fog over the few buildings, vacant lots. He could smell the Hudson two blocks over. He turned his footsteps east toward the large nine-story structure half buried by the fog and night.

He used a crowbar on the back door. The alarm never went off. A shorter—put together from a diagram in the Chairman's mind—froze the system.

Inside, Block used a flashlight, played it along the dusty floor. He found the crates he wanted, some twenty minutes later, on the warehouse's third floor. They were marked Intra-Flex, one of the World-Wide fronts. It had taken the *Register* crew only a few hours of steady digging to find this location. And to pass the information on to Block.

Block pried a crate open, pulled out a computer part. He triggered the autohypno key in his mind to the proper subject matter, removed a miniature tool kit from his coat pocket, began to disassemble the product.

"You *what*?" Block said.

"Got the job last Tuesday," Nora said.

"Jesus."

"It wasn't easy," Nora said. "Daisy Ltd. didn't need a secretary; they had plenty of their own."

"You just showed up and asked them?"

"Of course not."

Block pushed away his empty dinner plate, reached for the half-full wineglass. The voices of nighttime SoHo revelers came through the partly open window. He said, "So?"

"Phoned them. No openings. Then I went over to their office on East thirty-eighth Street. About four-thirty. They're on the third floor. There was a ladies' room down the hall, only it was locked. But a fat woman from some other office used it—had the key—and I went in with her."

"The CIA lost a great agent when you decided to go out on your own," Block said.

"Don't scoff, it gets even better. From the ladies' room I could keep an eye on Daisy. Four forty-five the office personnel start heading home. I picked out a middle-aged, chubby woman and followed her down in the elevator."

Block emptied his wineglass. "She turned out to be a secretary?"

"Of course."

"How'd you know?"

"By the way she was dressed, silly. Gimbel's bargain basement special. Simply no way to mistake it vice-presidential attire, if you know what I mean?"

"Uh-huh. Then what?"

"I approached her, bribed her, and got her job for a week."

"Just like that?"

"Took some doing, of course. Told her I was doing a research piece on computer companies for my college course. Not the technology side, but what it's like to work for one. Business 1004. Offered her a paid vacation for one week. Gave her five hundred dollars. That's three hundred more than she earns. She called up her boss next morning, said she had the flu, but that her cousin could sub for her. I didn't give them my real name, of course. And I've been an employee ever since."

Block sighed, shook his head. "Right into the hornet's nest."

"It's a *very* dull place to be, Ross. Nothing happens there but sales. Lots of forms to fill out, plenty of filing, stuff like that. The personnel couldn't be any more docile or boring."

"Docile?"

"Don't be jealous, Ross, just because I'm a better investigator than you are. I'm doing it for *you*."

"Thanks loads. Listen, I broke into their warehouse last night."

"Daisy Ltd.?"

"Uh-huh. Only they were using the name Intra-Flex. Same thing. Took apart some of their computers. Guess what? They have them rigged. Products going all over the world. But there's a device in each that lets outside parties tap in, disrupt the computer at will, give it different orders even. You understand what I'm saying? These babies are bound for Russia, China, Germany, France, the United States. It's no secret where they're going. Government offices. Military bases. The space program. They're advanced models, more than a step or two ahead of the competition, tailor-made for top-priority projects and dirt-cheap. That's what gives them their edge, gets them into the right places. Hastings and his bunch are playing for keeps, Nora; the stakes don't come any higher. Calling them dangerous is putting it mildly. And you've gone and walked right into their hands."

"Ross, since when are you a computer expert?"

"Hidden talents."

"No kidding? And all these experts, these military types and their scientists who are ordering these machines, don't realize what they're getting?"

"No."

"They're stupid."

"Could be."

"Ross—"

"Maybe they don't know what to look for. And wouldn't recognize it if they saw it."

"And you would?"

"Uh-huh."

"Sweetie—"

Block raised a hand. "I know what I know, honey. I can't explain how—not yet, anyway—but I do. You've got to take it on faith."

"You're a real pain, Ross."

"I realize that."

"An extremely exasperating person."

"I admit it. But you've got to quit this job. As of now. Don't even go back, you understand? I have enough on my mind without worrying about you, honest to God. Just vanish from that office."

"Okay. I've found out as much as I can, anyway. But I'm going to give you a break."

"Yes?"

"I can see you know everything already, so this will probably come as no surprise, but I'll give it to you just the same. To show I wasn't wasting my time at Daisy. Remember Paul Draden, the head clerk at McCoy for fifteen years? The one who gave you all that alleged dope on his former bosses?"

"Uh-huh."

"Well, if Hastings is behind Daisy Ltd., as you claim, then Hastings is still his boss. Paul Draden signed on as a consultant two days ago."

"You listen to me," Joe Sullivan said. "By the time we're through with you, Draden, your name's gonna be a household world."

Joe Sullivan was a large, stocky, balding man with watery blue eyes and a mild manner; twenty muck-raking years on the *Register* had taught him how to disguise his true nature with little difficulty.

Sullivan shook his finger at a pale-faced Draden. "You're in this up to your neck, Draden. You were head clerk at McCoy, one of Hasting's right-hand boys. You said Hastings left you and the company high and dry. You even spilled your guts to one of our reporters. You made yourself look good, Draden, but all that was nothing more than an act, a cover-up. You're back with Hastings at Daisy Ltd. Quintex controlled both McCoy and Daisy. And your boss controls the lot. You're in his pocket, Draden, the *Register*'s gonna put a spotlight on you both."

Draden said, "Drag me through the mud, Mr. Sullivan, and your paper will find itself faced with a multimillion-dollar lawsuit."

"We'll prove every word of it, Draden."

Sullivan pulled a miniature camera from his pocket; it flashed three times.

Draden had only managed to partially cover his face. "Get out!" he screamed.

"You'll be hearing from me," Sullivan said.

He got out.

Block sat in the car, waited. He saw Sullivan step out of the brownstone, turn west toward Lexington, fade into the night.

Block flipped on the audio-dip, aimed it toward Draden's first-floor apartment.

The sound was fuzzy at first, grew clearer when Block adjusted the range. He heard a telephone being dialed. It rang twice.

"Yeah?"

"It's me."

"Go on."

"There have been some developments," Draden's voice said.

"So?"

"I must make immediate contact."

"Kinda tough just now."

"This is an emergency."

"You sure?"

Draden sounded annoyed. "Sure I'm sure."

"I'll haveta call you back."

"When?"

"A couple hours."

"As fast as you can."

"Yeah."

The phone went click.

Block put the audio-dip on the seat next to him, still tied to Draden's line. He turned on WNCN. The Brahms clarinet quintet came through the speaker. Block folded his arms over his chest, stretched out his legs, and settled down for an extended wait.

The phone in Draden's flat rang again some seventy minutes later. Draden picked it up.

"Okay," the voice said, "you got a meet."

"When?"

"Tonight."

"Where?"

"Staten Island Ferry. Eleven-thirty sharp. Make sure you ain't being tailed."

"Don't worry," Draden said.

Block grinned into the darkness, pulled away from the curb. He didn't have to shadow Draden through New York traffic, he could simply pick him up on the ferry. Simple. He was glad something was.

CHAPTER

22

The day was bright, clear, with a nip in the air.

I took a deep breath, turned, went back into the Fellowship's mountain retreat, closed the door softly behind me.

I'd been back a week now. Rava and I had made it across the border to the South with no great sweat. Some loose change had greased the way. It took us a few days to reach the lab. I didn't waste any time putting the transmitter together. The boys had done a swell job turning up the equipment; only a couple of items were missing. I jerry-rigged some substitutes. The fuel pile was the last part to fit into place.

This was the day.

"Ready?" Targ asked.

"As ready as I'll ever be."

We went down the hallway into a large, white-walled room. Rava and Casparian were already there. So was my makeshift transmitter.

"You'll be back?" the girl said.

"You've got my word on that."

"Your journey may be a difficult one," Casparian said.

"It's worth the risk."

"Good luck," he said.

Rava embraced me.

"We have put all our hopes on you," Targ said.

"Don't worry," I told him. "But even if I don't make it through the transmitter in one piece, never get back to you folks, you'll still be okay."

Targ shrugged.

"Look," I said, "you've got the inside track now, know the score, that South and North Xcroth are part of the same setup, nothing more than pawns in an old-fashioned power grab. And that Jilks and Nardlow are the same guy. You got enough contacts on both sides to put the idea over. Take it from me, it'll go like wildfire. Jilks and his crew won't last a day once they're exposed as stooges of an offworlder.

"The whole thing was Ganz's idea, a kind of holding action till he was ready to make his move, a stagnant social order that would be a pushover. Especially if his boys were in the top slots, kept there by an 'emergency' that wouldn't go away, by two armed camps holding down different parts of the globe and hating each other.

"But if there's one thing you guys on this planet hate even worse than each other, it's an offworlder. That's your ace. And that's what I'm counting on."

I nodded, stepped on the platform, grinned at them, turned some knobs.

Blackness came and carried me away.

CHAPTER

23

Fog rolled over the water, thick and impenetrable. Deep-throated foghorns sent a mournful dirge into the night. Lights were dim smudges in the distance.

Block stood on the deck of the ferry, a solitary figure lost in the shadows, and felt the boat rock under his feet.

Small voices sounded in his ear, transmitted by the two-inch audio-dip he held in his palm. It was trained on a pair of almost invisible figures huddled near the boat's stern.

"Listen," Draden said, "they know *something*."

"Calm yourself," a shallow voice replied. "What could they possibly know?"

"Enough to connect me with Daisy Ltd."

"So?"

"Don't act dumb. Daisy is a link in the World-Wide chain. It can lead them to Quintex, and from there to all our European branches. Isn't that obvious?"

"Perhaps to you," the shallow voice said. "We are well covered."

"Not that well, Striker. It's only a matter of effort. Once their suspicions are aroused—"

"Try to control your anxiety, Draden. Do that for

me. Even if they stumbled over something now, how could they stop us before Birdwatch? Use your head. Afterward it will certainly not matter."

"You're wrong," Draden said.

"Yes? Tell me how."

"There's still a full week to go before Birdwatch—a full week!"

"So?"

"In the meantime they could move against us, dismantle our entire apparatus. Don't you see?"

Striker sighed. "Hardly. Even if this newspaper of yours published an exposé, what damage could possibly result? The authorities are not known for their impulsiveness. The week will pass quickly."

"They could arrest me, Striker; I wouldn't enjoy being questioned. Either would the others."

"So what do you suggest?"

"I disappear. Along with Frazer and Wald. We remove ourselves from the scene. Then let them write what they want. Daisy and Intra-Flex have served their purpose anyway."

"You are a bundle of nerves, Draden."

"Perhaps. You'll relay my request?"

"Of course."

"I'll be by my phone tonight."

"As you wish."

The pair of taillights were pale eyes, peering out of the fog. They turned a corner. Block turned after them.

The two cars seemed adrift in a sea of haze. Building tops vanished in the mist. Storefronts, streetlamps, and passing cars swam in and out of focus. Block pressed down on the gas pedal, drew closer to his quarry. He hummed a discordant tune to himself as he drove. In his mind he flipped through an index, one the Chairman had thoughtfully provided as a guide to his many crimes. Birdwatch appeared three times. It was the code word for totally destabilizing a planet. The Chairman had been successful all three times. Pabst had been his chief of operations twice. Block sighed, leaned back in his seat, and concentrated on the pair of taillights ahead of him.

The two-car procession cut a swath through the fog, traveled up Broadway past City Hall, along the drab stretch between Canal and Houston Streets, on to Fourteenth Street—dark and shuttered against the night—then westward past Gimbels and Macy's at Herald Square, and over to Times Square.

Striker turned left on Forty-second Street. It was 1:20 a.m. The live girlie shows, porno flicks, and B-movie houses were still doing a booming business. Marquees beckoned, blinked, and glittered. The good-time crowd filled the street.

The car ahead turned again, heading north along Eighth Avenue. Block went with it. There were more hookers here, more girlie shows and gay burlesque theaters. The avenue seemed even more squalid than Forty-second street. Refuse littered the pavements. The buildings seemed bleached and shabby.

Striker turned at Forty-eighth Street, parked between Eighth and Ninth.

Block drove past, turned the corner on Ninth Avenue, double-parked, hopped out of his car. Peering around the corner, he saw Striker enter a five-story tenement. The door swung shut behind him.

Block moved toward the building, halted a few houses down. He removed the audio-dip from his pocket, trained it on the tenement. His fingers began to adjust the range finder.

At least three people were using a phone in the tenement besides Striker. Block fiddled with the fine tuner.

Striker said, "The reporter was from the *Register*."

"Ross Block?" a voice asked.

Block recognized Pabst-Hastings.

"Not this time," Striker said. "A man named Sullivan. Draden is upset; he wants to disappear until after Birdwatch. And take Frazer and Wald with him."

"What do you think, Striker?"

"He has become a danger to us."

"I agree."

"He must be terminated."

"Yes."

"At once."

"I will personally handle this."

The line went click.

Block replaced the audio-dip, retreated to the corner, stopped in the shadows, and waited. The fog had turned to rain. A thin drizzle spattered the pavements. A lone foghorn sounded from the waterfront. Block put up the collar of his coat.

Striker stepped through the doorway of the tenement, headed for his car.

Block sprinted for his, climbed in, drove off, his foot pressing down hard on the gas pedal.

He ran three red lights before reaching Twenty-eighth Street and Lexington Avenue.

Draden was still fully dressed. An open bottle of scotch rested on an end table. Draden jumped up from his chair as the bell rang. A moment later Striker entered the apartment.

His coat was wet from the rain outside. He was bareheaded. He kept his hands in his pockets.

"I didn't expect you," Draden said. He seemed unsteady on his feet.

The two men moved to the center of the living room.

"The news I bring could not be relayed over the telephone," Striker said.

Draden nodded dumbly.

"It is as you wished," Striker said. "You are to go away on a short vacation."

Draden grinned drunkenly. "See? Knew what I was talking about."

Striker said, "You were given a list of contacts."

"Right."

"It still exists?"

Draden tapped his head with a finger. "Memorized."

"Ah," Striker said. And withdrew a revolver from his coat pocket.

Draden's face lost its grin.

"I am sorry," Striker said, sounding genuinely sorry.

"This is a mistake—" Draden began.

"It is no mistake," Striker said, raising his gun.

Ross Block, perched on a trash can in the alley next to Draden's window, shot Striker three times in the chest.

"They are everywhere," Draden said. His forehead was damp with perspiration, but his eyes were clear. Draden had sobered up fast. Block poured him another cup of coffee.

"Drink it," he said.

Draden raised the cup to his lips with shaking fingers, took a swallow.

Striker was stretched out in the darkened bedroom; he was dead. A green towel covered the bloodstains on the living-room rug.

Draden said, "You have no idea how far-reaching Birdwatch is."

"Sure I do," Block said. "Your boys had close to a decade to do their work. You infiltrated the top echelons of government. Science was your ticket to the top; some military systems, some hardware just a cut or two above the current generation. It opened the doors, and once an agent got in, he brought in the rest. That's it, Draden, isn't it? Birdwatch."

Draden's face paled. "You're one of them, aren't you?" he whispered.

"Uh-uh. Just that I know more about your Mr. Hastings than you do. And the way he operates."

"How could you?"

Block smiled pleasantly. "Ever wonder how Hastings came up with his scientific marvels?"

Draden shrugged.

"The same way I know what's going on."

"I don't understand."

"You're not supposed to. All you've got to understand is that I'm the one guy who can get you out alive."

"The police—"

"Aren't coming. This is a laser weapon; it's soundless. No one heard a thing."

"The body—"

"Will be gone by morning. You'll help me carry it to my car. I'll dump it in the East River. There's no way to connect you with Striker, is there?"

"No."

"Then you're in the clear. Except for Hastings and his boys. Your life's not worth a plugged nickel if they get their hands on you, is it?"

"I trusted Hastings."

"So did lots of people. Most are dead now. Don't join them, Draden."

"After Birdwatch they'll be in control. The computers Hastings built service all the superpowers. They can be tapped into, given wrong orders. They will signal enemy launchings, atomic attacks. Chaos will result. And Hastings's agents will sieze power."

"There isn't going to be any Birdwatch. Not if you

give me what you've got. I need names—all you can supply—addresses, dates, the works."

"And then?"

"You get lost, go hide somewhere. Let me handle this. I've got the means."

"I will," Draden said; his voice was shaking.

"Sure you will," Block said. "What choice've you got?"

The night closed around him. Rain pounded against car and windshield. Gravel crunched under his wheels. Another hour would see daylight.

Block turned in at the narrow dirt road, his wheels churning in the mud; the car crept slowly forward. Bushes and trees were on either side of the roadway.

Then the house sprang up in his headlights—weathered wood and shingles, windows and doors locked tight against the darkness.

Block sighed, killed the motor. He'd collected enough dope on Pabst to put a damper on his operation. He had the names, locations of the agents, could blow the whistle on the lot of them. Only Pabst and his inner circle were still missing. Draden ran the New York end, was savvy to the global setup too. But he didn't know Pabst's whereabouts, took his orders through Striker. And Striker was dead.

It didn't matter. Pabst would turn up sooner or later. The important thing was to squelch Birdwatch. Block couldn't do it alone, not in a week, at least, even if he gave the story to the press. But he wasn't alone, was he? The transmitter was stashed in that old house. He'd zip back to the Control World, pick up Siscoe and a couple hundred armed Galactic guards, return to Earth, and mop up the Pabst bunch. Sweet and simple.

Block climbed out of the car, waded through the mud until he reached the side of the building.

The window was as he'd left it.

He hoisted himself over the sill, moved quickly across creaking floorboards to the back of the house, pushed open a final door.

The old sofa with the jutting springs was still there. The broken chair lay on its side as before. Spiderwebs continued to decorate three corners of the wall. And the transmitter rested solidly on the floor.

What was new to the room were the three men.

Two were unfamiliar.

The third wasn't.

He had a jutting chin and red hair and wore a green parka.

Block recognized Lew Jenks, Pabst's chief flunky.

"Hiya, palsy," he said. And grinned. "Surprise."

All three held guns in their hands.

There was no signal between the three. No words were exchanged.

The guns opened fire on Block.

And the bullets exploded in midair.

"Don't kill them," the voice of Nick Siscoe said. "We're going to need them to lug the damn transmitter into your car."

The car rode through a wash of rain. Ross Block sat at the wheel. The transmitter was piled in the back seat. The three gunmen had been left behind in the house, their hands and feet bound with strips of their own clothing.

"It's only about a forty-five-minute ride," Nick Siscoe said.

"Why can't I see you?" Block asked.

"Because I'm not here," Siscoe said. "Ganz rigged the transmitter back on the Control World. I used it and landed on a backwoods world called Xcroth, one that Ganz had earmarked for a future takeover.

"They had a platform there, all right, but not the

rest of the gizmo. Ganz had given me a one-way ticket.

"I dug around in the Chairman's mind, put together a transmitter, and charted a course for the Control World. No dice. A black hole plays havoc with transmitters from Xcroth, distorts time as well as space. My body's somewhere in hyperspace. What got through is raw energy, a kind of electrical field. Watch."

In the seat next to Block a shape began to take form—a transparent, glowing Nick Siscoe.

"Jesus," Block said.

"Don't touch," Siscoe said. "You'll get burned. It's an energy flow, see? I can control it, shape it, even make it talk. As long as I stick close to the damn transmitter. If I get too far away I start to fade.

"You were waiting for me?" Block said.

"Yeah. In between a couple of side trips."

"You knew I'd show up?"

"Sooner or later. Especially once the goon squad arrived. They were laying for you, pal. I just sat tight, listened to 'em gab. They gave the whole play away. Pabst sent his top team right from HQ; I know how to get there now."

"How'd you manage the trick with the bullets?" Block asked.

"Easy. Just put a wall of energy in front of you. Blew up the bullets."

"Uh-huh," Block said. "I get all that. What I don't get is why we're going to take on Pabst all by ourselves. Why not ring in the Galactic guards, let them handle him?"

"A couple of reasons. Pabst couldn't crack your force lock, use the transmitter himself. But he made sure no one else would either. Thing's aimed into hyperspace. It'll take some time to set it right."

"So?" Block said. "We have a week."

"Had. That's the second item. Pabst's moved up his schedule."

"For when?"

"About sixty minutes from now."

"Turn left," Siscoe said.

The car wound its way up a gravel road. Trees rose straight into the darkness at the road's edge, stretched off into blackness. Rain wailed around them.

"Sure we're headed right?" Block said.

"Yeah. Listen, this is the play. We go up against Pabst, wreck him."

"Just like that?"

"Sure. You've got me along, haven't you?"

"You're not even a body, Nick."

"Yeah. But what I am is even better. You got the dope on Pabst's network?"

"Uh-huh."

"That's what Jenks figured. Glad you weren't sitting around on your duff all this time. Okay, between us we've got this thing sewed up."

"You're sure, eh?"

"Positive. We rope Pabst, fix up the transmitter, and beat it back to Xcroth. I know the way. Remember the side trips I mentioned? Been flipping back and forth between all the transmitter points. Cover 'em in about an eyeblink. So I got it mapped out now, know the route. All we got to do is dodge the time loop. We hit Xcroth. I show you how to bring back my body. Then we take off for the Control World—"

"Round up some guards," Block said, "return to Earth, and assassinate the rest of Pabst's bunch."

"Right on target, Ross. Knock 'em off. That way we *know* they won't be up to mischief. Then we go looking for Ganz."

"You make it sound easy, Nick."

"It will be."

The red brick structure was cylindrical, weathered, with giant cracks in its walls.

Two small windows gave off a dim light.

"There she is," the voice of Nick Siscoe said. "An old power station. Out in the middle of nowhere. He's been here all along setting up his gear. Push a button and you get World War Three. Neat."

"What do we do, just walk in?"

"Yeah, that's what we do. Only I'll be in front, a solid wall of energy. You come in blasting away."

"I shoot through you?"

"I'll make an opening, stupid."

"Not too wide, eh?"

"Don't worry, pal, just mow 'em down. I'll do the rest."

The door was locked.

Block stepped back in the rain, used his laser.

The lock turned red, white, split in two.

Block kicked open the door.

There were two of them in the outer room.

Block fired and got the first.

A machine gun swung at him. The short, stubby man pressed hard on the trigger.

Bullets beat against an invisible wall, exploded.

"Now," Nick Siscoe said.

Through Siscoe's opening, Block sent a beam into the man's chest. He crashed to the floor.

"Up the stairs," Siscoe said.

Block took him three at a time.

A tall figure appeared at the head of the stairs. Two guns blazed in his hands. A wave of electric energy sent the man toppling.

"Next landing," Siscoe said.

Block's feet carried him up to the third floor.

Two men sprang at him from a side corridor, screamed as a wave of electricity shot through them, convulsed, and died.

"I'm getting the hang of this," Nick Siscoe said. "It's fun."

"Over there," Block said.

A solitary figure stood framed in a doorless archway.

He was slender, his face long and narrow, lips thin, nose flat.

Pabst-Hastings.

Behind him, running up the length of the wall and out of sight beyond the archway, hardware glittered in the white light. Dials, gauges, knobs; a tangle of multicolored wire strands climbed the giant computer like some plastic vine.

The thin lips smiled. Pabst spoke. "Still a meddler. Too bad. Should have run, Block, when you had the chance."

Block fired.

White heat leaped from his laser. And defused in midair.

"Force field," Nick Siscoe said.

Pabst stepped out of view.

"The button," Block said. "He's going to push it."

"Not if I get there first. I can cross the field. Get down. There may be fireworks."

Block ducked.

The floor moved under his feet. A huge thunder-clap seemed to envelop him. The wall buckled. A black wave swept down on him.

Block groaned, tried to sit up.

He was stretched out on the floor, half buried under concrete and rubble.

Daylight shone through large cracks in the wall.

"Nick," Block heard himself say through swollen lips.

No answer.

Slowly, painfully, Block moved in the rubble, climbed shakily to his feet.

He could barely stand.

He staggered toward the archway, went through it.

The computer was a fused and charred ruin. Part of it had melted, spilled onto the floor.

"Jesus," Block muttered.

There were no bodies, no sign of Pabst.

"Nick," Block said.

He turned slowly, and after what seemed a very long time managed to make his way down three flights of stairs and outdoors.

It had stopped raining.

The car and transmitter were gone.

Block sighed, and began hobbling down the still muddy road.

Siscoe had nipped Birdwatch, all right, but the price—for him—had been higher than expected.

And who the hell had made off with the car and transmitter?

Block would reach the city, hand over his evidence—his list of names, Pavel's files, Draden's documents—to the *Register*. With no button to press, with Birdwatch blown to kingdom come, Pabst's agents would be sitting ducks. The feds, Interpol, the Sûrété, the KGB would do Block's work for him. It might take time, but there *was* time now.

Somehow he'd build another transmitter, get back to the Control World.

Somehow . . .

About the Author

Isidore Haiblum was born in Brooklyn, New York. He attended CCNY, edited the college humor magazine, *Mercury*, took honors in Yiddish, and graduated with a B.A. in English. He has published ten science fiction novels, including *The Tsaddik of the Seven Wonders, Transfer to Yesterday, The Mutants Are Coming*, and *The Identity Plunderers*, available in a Signet edition. He was also co-author of a book about the golden age of radio. His many articles dealing with Yiddish, popular culture, and humor have appeared in such publications as *Twilight Zone* magazine and the *Village Voice*. His novels have been translated into French, German, Hebrew, Italian, and Spanish. He lives and works in New York City.

Great Science Fiction from SIGNET